Banished and Forgotten

Irish Slaves in the West Indies

Louise Gherasim, M.A

authorHOUSE®

AuthorHouse™
1663 Liberty Drive, Suite 200
Bloomington, IN 47403
www.authorhouse.com
Phone: 1-800-839-8640

First published by AuthorHouse 6/15/2009

ISBN: 978-1-4389-7563-4 (sc)

Printed in the United States of America
Bloomington, Indiana

This book is printed on acid-free paper.

This is a historical novel set in the 17th century and based on the little known story of the Irish slaves in the West Indies and Virginia. These men, women and children were rounded up by Cromwell's soldiers and shipped in trading vessels to the sugar and tobacco plantations which were then owned by the English.
Maps – courtesy of Michael Gherasim

"Natural liberty is the gift of the beneficent Creator of the whole human race."

- Alexander Hamilton

Dedication

To Ireland and the Irish people, a long-suffering and heroic race. Now in the 21st century, they have at last prospered. Having thrown off the English yolk, they have risen to become a highly educated and wealthy nation.

Acknowledgements

First of all, I must thank my son, Gabriel, for all his help with the research for this book.

Thanks to Joyce Niewendorp and other members of the Tigard Library.

Thanks to Madeleine Brink for the typing of the book.

Thanks to Angela Rosemeyer for her editing skills and graphic design.

And last but not least, my beloved husband, Teodor, who never ceases to encourage and support me.

Historical Characters

<u>Oliver Cromwell</u> (1599 – 1658)

Oliver Cromwell was an English military and political leader. He is best known for his part in making England a Republican Commonwealth. During the English Civil War, he was one of the commanders of the New Model Army who defeated the royalists. After King Charles I was executed in 1649, it was Cromwell who ruled the short-lived Commonwealth of England. He devastated Ireland and also ruled Scotland as Lord Protector from 1653 to his death in 1658.

Born into the ranks of the middle gentry, Cromwell was relatively unknown for the first forty years of his life. During the 1630s he had a religious conversion to a Puritan life-style. He was elected Member of Parliament for Cambridge in the Short 1640 and Long 1640-49 Parliaments. He later became involved in the Civil War on the side of the 'Roundheads' or Parliamentarians.

He was a brilliant soldier, rising from the rank of leading a single cavalry troop to commander of the whole army. He quickly became known as 'Old Ironsides.' In 1649, he signed the death warrant for Charles I. Later that same year, he was chosen by Parliament to lead a campaign in Ireland. The following year, he led an army against Scotland. Then in April 1653, he dismissed Parliament and set up a short-lived assembly known as the Barebones Parliament. Thereafter, he was declared Lord Protector of England.

Cromwell and Ireland

Cromwell hated the Irish. This hatred was both political and religious. He was passionately opposed to the Catholic Church, which he saw as denying the primacy of the Bible in favor of papal and clerical authority. He also blamed Catholicism for the persecution of Protestants throughout Europe.

Since 1641, the English Parliament had planned to re-conquer Ireland and had sent an invasion army into the country. After the civil war in England ended, Cromwell was able to command a much larger force, and in 1649 he landed in Dublin and immediately attacked the fortified port towns of Drogheda and Wexford. In Drogheda alone his troops massacred 3,500 people. In Wexford 2,000 Irish troops and 1,500 civilians were sacrificed while much of the town was burned. One town after another was treated in the same way.

Following a three-year conquest of Ireland, the Catholic religion was banned and priests were executed when captured. All had a price on their heads. Thousands upon thousands of Irish people were sold into slavery. All Catholic-owned land was confiscated in the Act for the Settlement of Ireland 1652, and given to Scottish and English settlers, the Parliamentary soldiers or Parliament's financial creditors. Under the Commonwealth, Catholic land ownership dropped from 60% to 8%.

Although Cromwell himself did not spend a great deal of time in Ireland, his commanders in the field continued his handiwork. 'To Hell or to Connaught' was the cry heard across the country. Connaught was the most depressed and poorest land in Ireland at the time. It was to this part of the country that those who survived were ordered to go. In modern Ireland the phrase is still synonymous with a 'choice' in which there is no choice at all.

Ann Glover

Born in Ireland, Ann Glover was shipped into slavery by Oliver Cromwell. She was sent to Barbados in the 1650s. Her story unfolds in the pages of my book.

Members of the McCarthy family were, of course, historical figures holding power and wealth from time immemorial to the 17th century when their power and influence were destroyed by the English invaders. Their lands and castles were located in southwestern Ireland.

Other historical personages include Roger Osborne, Governor of Barbados, and Governor General of all the English Leeward Islands, as well as his successor, Sir William Stapleton.

Forward

"Qui Angliam vincere vellet ab Ibernia incipere debet."
"Who would England win in Ireland must begin."

Ireland in the 17th Century

Having poisoned Owen Roe O'Neill, one of the greatest military leaders of the era, the English were now free to do their worst in Ireland.

> "Did they dare, did they dare to slay
>   Eoghan Ruadh O'Neill?
> Yes, they slew with poison him they feared
>   to meet with steel.
> May God wither up their hearts!
> May their blood cease to flow!
> May they walk a living death, who poisoned
>   Eoghan Ruadh."
>   -   Thomas Davis.

Cromwell landed in Dublin in the summer of 1640 with a Puritan army of seventeen thousand. These Ironsides, as they were called, were fiercely fanatical. They hated the Papists and considered themselves chosen by God to take over the land of Ireland and destroy its people – "the idol-worshipping Canaanites who were cursed by God." In order to inspire the army to even greater heights of animosity, Puritan preachers of the Word sailed with the troops and constantly reminded them of the papistical Irish. Men, such as Hugh Peters and Stephen Jerome, "preached a war of extermination in the most startling and fearsome manner – in the pulpit invoking the curse of God upon those who should hold back their hands from slaying 'while man, woman or child of Belial remains alive.' Peters exhorted his hearers to do as did the conquerors of Jericho, 'Kill all that were, young men and old, children and maidens.'"

With words such as these ringing in their ears, the Ironsides attacked the town of Drogheda on the Boyne River some 30 miles north of Dublin. The horrendous scene that followed can best be described by the Englishman Carlyle: "Oliver Cromwell came as a soldier of God the Just, terrible as Death, relentless as Doom doing God's judgments on the enemies of God..." Arthur Wood, the Oxford historian, gives us another account based on the writing of his brother who was an officer in Cromwell's army. "Each of the assistants would take a child and use it as a buckler of defense to keep him from being shot or brained. After they had killed all in the streets, they did likewise in the churches. They then went down to the vaults underground where all the choicest of women had hid themselves. One of these, a most handsome virgin, arrayed in costly and gorgeous apparel, knelt down to Wood, with tears and prayers begging him for her life; and being stricken with a profound pity, he did take her under his arm for the works, to shift for herself, but a soldier, perceiving his intention ran the sword through her, whereupon Mr. Wood, seeing her gasping, took away her money, jewels etc., and flung her down over the works."

After the town was completely destroyed, and its inhabitants slaughtered, the Primate of Ireland, Oliver Plunkett, was shackled and taken to England. There he was lodged in The Tower, interrogated, tortured and finally hung, drawn and quartered. His head was severed from his body and placed on a spike on The Tower walls so that all might see the fate of those who refused to embrace the Puritan Credo.

Cromwell sent the following letter to the speaker of the House of Commons in England: "It has pleased God to bless our endeavor at Drogheda... the enemy were about 3000 strong in the town. I believe we put to the sword the whole number... This hath been a marvelous great mercy... I wish that all honest hearts may give the glory of this to God alone, to whom indeed the praise of this mercy belongs." And later, "In this very place (St. Peter's Church) a thousand of them were put to the sword, fleeing thither for safety....And now give me leave to say how this work was wrought. It was set upon some of our hearts that a great thing should be done, not by power or might, but by the spirit of God. And is it not so, clearly?"

In response, the English Parliament appointed a national Thanksgiving Day in celebration of the dreadful slaughter – and by unanimous vote placed upon the Parliamentary records, "That the House does approve of the execution done at Drogheda as an act of both justice to them (the butchered ones) and mercy to others who may be warned by it."

Having reduced the other towns in the area in like manner, Cromwell turned his attention to the South. He marched on Wexford, eliminating the garrisons of Arklow, Enniscorthy and Ross on his way.

The tragedy of events in Drogheda was repeated in Wexford. MacManus states in his book, *The Story of the Irish Race*, that two thousand were butchered there. And he continues, to assert that Cromwell "thought it a simple act of justice to 'the Saints,' his soldiers, to indulge them in the little joy of slaughtering the Canaanites." Cromwell made "no distinction between the defenseless inhabitants and the armed soldiers, nor could the shrieks and prayers of three hundred females who had gathered round the great Cross in the market-place, preserve them from the swords of these ruthless barbarians," as stated by Lingard in his *History of England*.

Continuing west to Waterford and then on to Cork, Cromwell and his Ironsides took the cities with relative ease as they were garrisoned by English Protestants who readily sold out to their countrymen. In return they were rewarded with large grants of Irish lands in the North.

Priests, monks and nuns were singled out and tortured before they were put to death. The Bishop of Ross had his hands and feet cut off before he was hanged. A young priest captured in Arklow was tied to a wild horse's tail and dragged to the town of Gorey some ten miles further south.

Cromwell in summing up the situation after the siege of Waterford told the President of the Council of State, John Bradshaw: "I believe there was lost of the enemy not many less than two thousand and I believe not twenty of yours killed, from first to last of the siege."

Shortly thereafter, Cromwell returned to England leaving his general, Ireton, to carry on his 'good' work. The carnage continued for several years until in May 1652 the Articles of Kilkenny signed by the Parliamentary Commissions and the Earl of West Meath officially terminated the "longest, the most appallingly dreadful and inhumane, and the most exhausting war, with which unfortunate Ireland was ever visited."

One would expect that peace would now settle in the land but that was not the case. The book, *Life of Bishop Kirwan,* by Lynch, describes the plight of those who were left alive: "Along with three scourges of God, famine, plague and war there was another which some called the fourth scourge, to wit, the weekly exaction of the soldiers' pay, which was extorted with incredible atrocity, each Saturday – bugles sounding, and drums beating. On these occasions the soldiers entered the various houses, and pointing their muskets to the breasts of men and women threatened them with instant death if the sum demanded was not immediately given. Should it have so happened that the continual payment of these taxes had exhausted the means of the people, bed, bedding, sheets, table-clothes, dishes and every description of furniture, nay, the very garments of the women, torn off their persons, were carried to the market-place and sold for a small sum; so much so, that each recurring Saturday bore a resemblance to the Day of Judgment…"

'To Hell or to Connaught'

The worst was yet to come. The wars had ended but peace did not follow. The exhausted nation was again set upon by the followers of Cromwell and condemned to a fate worst than death – the terrible exile of countless families. Torn from their lands, their homes and all they knew, they were forced, with a few belongings, to leave the Provinces of Ulster, Leinster and Munster and repair to the bogs and barren mountainsides of Connaught. This forced evacuation, known as the great Cromwellian Settlement, was devised so that the fertile lands of Ireland might be given to the children of the conquerors.

Those who refused to leave the lands of their forefathers, or who sought to fight rather than be transported, were given one last option. They could join many of their countrymen in the service of foreign powers friendly to England. Thirty-five hundred under Colonel Edmund O'Dwyer went to the French Prince Condé: five thousand under Lord Muskerry, to the King of Poland; and about thirty thousand to the King of Spain.

But as these young men sailed for foreign parts, mothers, wives and children were left behind to grieve and fend for themselves in a hostile wasted land.

In time, these exiled Irish, according to one historian, rose to prominent positions in all walks of life. "They became Chancellors of universities, professors, and high officials in every European state. A Kerry-man became physician to Sobieski, King of Poland. A Donegal man was physician to the Privy Chancellor of the King of France and a very famed professor of medicine in the university of Toulouse and Bologna."

While Ireland's sons won exiled fame and fortune on the Continent as "Field Marshals, Admirals, Ambassadors, Prime Ministers, Scholars, Physicians, Merchants, Soldiers and Founders of mining industry," their mothers, wives, and children were being rounded up, dispossessed of all their belongings and shipped as slaves to the American colonies and the West Indies.

When Jamaica was acquired in 1655, the governor of the island asked for a thousand girls from Ireland to be sent

– "to the most appalling kind of slavery." And in a letter dated September 18, 1655, Henry of the Uprighte Harte, writing from Kilkenny to Secretary Thurloe states: "I think it might be of like advantage to your affairs there, and to ours heer, if you should thinke fitt to sende 1500 or 2000 young boys of from twelve to fourteen years of age, to the place aforementioned."

The pitiful state of affairs in Ireland after Cromwell's soldiers had done their worst can best be described by Prendergast in his *Cromwellian Settlement of Ireland.* He says: "Ireland in the language of Scripture, lay void as a wilderness. Five-sixths of her people had perished. Women and children were found daily perishing in ditches, starved. The bodies of many wandering orphans, whose fathers had been killed or exiled, and whose mothers had died of famine, were preyed upon by wolves. In the years 1652 and 1653, the plague, following the desolating wars, had swept away whole counties, so that one might travel twenty or thirty miles and not see a living creature. Man, beast and bird were all dead, or had quit those desolate places."

But somehow, the loyal servants of Oliver Cromwell found or hunted down thousands of displaced people: men, women and children and hounded them to the southern ports. Reverend Thomas Quin S.J. who had managed to avoid capture wrote a report to Rome giving an account of Irish Catholics from 1652-1656. "I believe that some 60,000 were sent there (Barbados); the husbands expelled first to Spain and the Netherlands, whilst the wives and offspring were destined for America, such that there was a perpetual divorce; thus what God and nature had joined, the barbarous tyranny of the heretics separated."

Others state that between 80,000 and 100,000 were shipped to the sugar plantations of Barbados alone. But other islands: St. Kitts, Nevis and Montserrat also became home to Irish slaves and indentured servants, the latter serving their masters without remuneration for seven to ten years in the case of adults but children were bound for much longer periods of time.

"Cromwell did more, however, in audacity, his attempt to reorder Ireland was as great as Joseph Stalin's rearrangement of the ethnic groups of the Soviet Union." According to Donald Harman Akenson in his book *If the Irish Ran the World*: "Cromwell divided the country into a patchwork of three categories of land: those where the existing arrangements were to be retained (held by people who had either by luck or conviction ended up on the winning side in the multi-sided Irish civil war); those where lands were confiscated, either in whole or part, and reserved for Puritan adventurers and their army, or by the Government for further allocation; and those counties beyond the Shannon to which Catholics were to be transported and required to settle. It was nothing less than a reconfiguration of the map of Ireland." He continues: "All social levels were affected, landlords down to churls".

This period in Irish history just described really started with the reign of Elizabeth I. "Had she lived in the 20th Century, she would have been viewed with the same horror as Hitler and Stalin." These are the words of James F. Cavanaugh of the Clann Chief Herald, who continues: "Her policy of Irish genocide was pursued with such evil zest it boggles the mind of modern men. But Elizabeth was only setting the stage for the even more savage program that was to follow her, directed specifically to exterminate the Irish.

James II and Charles I continued Elizabeth's campaign but Cromwell almost perfected it. Few people in modern so-called 'civilized history' can match the horrors of Cromwell in Ireland. It is amazing what one man can do to his fellow men under the banner that God sanctions his actions.

"Few people today realize that from 1600 to 1699 far more Irish were sold as slaves than Africans. Some 52,000 Irish, women, boys and girls were sold to Barbados and Virginia alone. Another 30,000 Irish men and women were taken prisoners and ordered transported and sold as slaves....As horrendous as these numbers sound, it only reflects a small part of the evil program, as most of the slaving activity was not recorded...

"However, from 1625 onward the Irish were sold, pure and simple, as slaves....They were captured and originally turned over to shippers to be sold for their profit. Because the profits were so great, generally 900 pounds of cotton for a slave, the Irish slave trade became an industry in which everyone involved (except the Irish) had a share of the profits..."

Mr. James F. Cavanaugh – Clann Chief Herald – writes of this period:

"Curiously, of all the Irish shipped out as slaves, not one is known to have returned to Ireland to tell their tales. Many, if not most, died on the ships transporting them or from overwork and abusive treatment on the plantations.... On the island of Montserrat, seven of every ten whites were Irish...

"There were horrendous abuses by the slavers, both to Africans and Irish. The records show that the British ship *Zong* was delayed by storms, and as their food was running low, they decided to dump 132 slaves overboard to drown so the crew would have plenty to eat. If the slaves died due to 'accident,' the loss was covered by insurance, but not if they starved to death."

Finally, Cavanaugh asks the question: "What were the Cavanaughs doing in Barbados?" He responds: "The answer takes us down a revolting path wandering through one of the most insensitive and savage episodes in history, where the greed and avarice of the English monarchy systematically planned the genocide of the Irish, for commercial profit, and executed a continuing campaign to destroy all traces of Irish social culture and religious being. As the topic was politically sensitive, little has been written about this attempted genocide of the Irish, and what has been written has been camouflaged because it is an ugly and painfully brutal story. But the story should be told."

With these words in mind and my own sense of justice for my longsuffering and oppressed nation, I have planned the following story.

It was under conditions such as those described that Sheila McCarthy and the young woman who befriended her, Ann 'Goody' Glover were rounded up with over two hundred other young boys and girls. The were bound together in pairs and shipped off to the West Indies to spend the rest of their lives as slaves in sugar and tobacco plantations.

Barbados

Of all the islands of the Caribbean, Barbados has perhaps the most unusual history. To begin, it was one of the few islands not 'discovered' by Columbus. It was a desolate place when an English settlement was established there in 1627. The island was named by some Portuguese sailors traveling under Pedro a Compoz in 1536 – Los Barbados or 'the land of the Bearded Fig Tree.' It is a coral island of approximately 166 square miles. Without mountains, it is non-volcanic and came into being some 750 thousand years ago.

Colonized by England in 1625, it had remained in English hands, known as 'Little England' until 1966.

Barbados is the nearest Caribbean island to Africa, hence it became the main entry-port for African slaves, later shipped to other territories.

The island is now the home of two main ethnic groups, the Africans and Irish, with a small minority of English who were originally overlords and slave-traders.

The African slaves were brought to the island beginning in the 1620s by the English. By 1645 the black population was 5,680 and by 1667 it had grown to over 40,000. Barbados also became the destination for military prisoners and Irishmen, women and children during Oliver Cromwell's reign. He it was who 'barbadosed' Irish who refused to clear off their own lands and allow English soldiers to occupy them. These rebels were then sold as slaves to English planters. The estimated number transported varies from 60,000 to 120,000 prisoners.

The colony was not without its problems. Spanish and French pirates raided the island and terrorized the slaves.

Turbulent weather conditions – hurricanes for the most part – decimated crops and gave the Irish and African slaves an opportunity to revolt. It also added to the image of the Irish as being 'wild savages' as they often instigated the attacks on the white slave owners in times of uncontrollable weather.

Today the kidnapped Irish have disappeared into history. What remained after an 1880 census was a small population of poor whites, whom the locals often called 'Redshanks.'

Montserrat

A mountainous and volcanic island set in the inner arc of the Leeward chain of the Lesser Antilles, Montserrat was first colonized by Europeans in the 1630s. Continual volcanic activity results in the frequent eruption of small boiling and bubbling lakes and hot springs. The best known, Hot Water Pond is situated on the western coast.

The island is approximately 39 1/2 square miles and is shaped like a 'tear drop.' Maybe this is significant. Only God knows how many tears were shed in that land of slaves and indentured servants.

There are few good landing places, except on the north-western coast where two small inlets interrupt the precipitous coast line. The soil is, for the most part, sandy particularly on the low levels while the mountain slopes are clayey.

The climate is tropical and the temperature varies from a high of 87° F in August to a low of 74° F in January. The humidity ranges from between 70 and 80 percent. The wettest months are September to December, while the driest period stretches from January to July.

The mountains support rainforests, and an abundance of mosses and lichens. Sage brush and cacti as well as 'Acacia savannah' have a home on the lower areas.

The beaches have black sand. The scenery is beautiful with creepers and bushes. The wildlife is modest – bats, birds, frogs and reptiles complete the list. But mention should be made of the black and yellow oriole, the national bird, which is found only in Montserrat.

The Taino Indians, who came from Venezuela, settled in the island as early as 200 AD. When Columbus visited

Montserrat in 1493 it was the Caribs who held sway there. They did not, actually, inhabit the island but used it as a base from time to time. A large garden high in the mountains indicates their previous inhabitance.

The second group of Europeans visited the area around 1631 under the leadership of Sir Henry Colt. By 1632 or 1633 an English settlement was established. For the next hundred years it was an English colony run and peopled mostly by persons from Ireland.

It was Columbus who named the island after Santa Maria de Monserrate monastery in the Catalan mountains where Ignatius Loyola later founded the Jesuits.

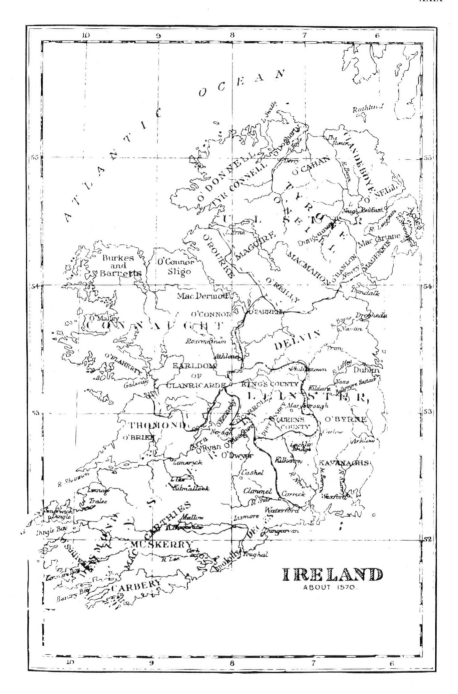

IRELAND
ABOUT 1570.

Ireland, Mother Ireland

Oh, land of love and beauty,
To you our hearts are wed.
To you in lowly duty
We ever bow our heads.
Oh, perfect loving Mother,
Your exiled children all
Across the sundry seas
To you in fond devotion call.

If you sigh, we hear you,
If you weep, we weep.
In your hours of gladness
How our pulses leap.
Ireland, Mother Ireland,
Whatever may befall,
Ever shall we hold you,
Dearest, best of all.

Dear isle across the ocean,
Dear loving land of ours,
May your days be sunny,
And your way a way of flowers.
Wide though we be scattered,
O'er alien vale or hill.
All the love you gave us
We keep and cherish still.

- P.J. O'Reilly

Part I

Chapter 1

"Whatever makes a man a slave takes half his worth away."

- Pope

Eóghan McCarthy, Lord of Muskerry, stood on the steps of his castle home and watched his children at play. The twittering of the birds and the rippling waters of a nearby stream mingled with the children's laughter. He stretched himself to his full height of six feet and surveyed the lush meadows stretching out towards the distant hills. It was good to be alive, good to be part of the rich valley he called his own.

A man of sturdy build, his sandy-red hair fell in waves to his shoulders. His blue-grey eyes twinkled and fairly danced with merriment beneath his broad brow when in the company of friends but froze to steel when the enemy was encountered. A firm determined jaw and generous mouth led no one to mistake his words. Eóghan McCarthy's laughter was infectious and his sense of humour wry. A man of action, he wasted little time in idle chatter.

He and his family enjoyed a relatively peaceful existence despite the rumblings and rumours of unrest in other parts of the country.

His attention was drawn to his oldest child, his daughter Sheila, and he exulted thinking of the beautiful woman she would become one day. Even now, her delicate features, her deep blue eyes, an abundance of golden hair cascading in ringlets to her slender waist, and shapely lips, red as the summer rose, gave ample testimony to his prediction.

But then he paused as he contemplated the character of the child he loved so much. She had, from infancy, displayed qualities he did not admire – a definite stubborn tendency – headstrong and argumentative. Yes, indeed, he concurred with his previous assessment of what he considered serious flaws in an otherwise beguiling and delightful child. He would have to draw the attention of those responsible for her education to these unacceptable traits. She was still young; time and discipline would surely curb her ill-humoured and contrary ways.

"Sheila, *a grád*," he audibly voiced, then nodded still holding council with himself, "May God bless you and keep you in His care."

Then he raised his tone: "Sheila, Sheila, come."

He anticipated the happy smile and the eager strides as the young girl raced to his outstretched arms.

"*M'athair!*" she cried, as she threw herself into his wide embrace. "I love you so much. I'm so glad you're home again. Please, don't go away anymore."

Eóghan smiled tenderly at his lovely daughter. You're becoming quite a young woman. Growing up too fast, *a cuisla mo croid*." He held her at arms length and looked her up and down. "'Tis looking for a husband for you, I'll be ere long." Then he ran his fingers through her tangled curls as the smaller children bounded up the castle steps.

There would be a banquet in the great hall that evening. The bard, O'Faolán, would entertain and add to his tales of bygone days the most recent achievements of The McCarthy, chieftain of all the lands of Muskerry, all 232,300 acres which had been handed down from many generations. In 1448 Cormac Laidin McCarthy inherited the title Lord of Muskerry. He did much to improve the existing castle, rebuilding and enlarging it. He also built a castle at Carrigadrohid and founded an Abby at Kilcrea. But his most notable achievement was the building of the Blarney Castle in 1446.

This night the mead would flow and the warriors who had fought at McCarthy's side would sing his praises and Sheila knew all would be well in her castle home.

She pictured her pretty mother dressed in fine 'silk,' a band of gold around her swan-like neck, her auburn tresses held in place by a diadem of emeralds set in gold. How beautiful she would appear seated by her handsome husband on the high dais. And Sheila also knew she would contribute to the pride of The McCarthy Clan when her beloved father called upon her to render a song of her own. Then she would climb upon the dais, and sitting close to her father's chair display her skill upon the harp as she accompanied herself.

From participating in these celebrations no one would be denied. Nor were there seating arrangements, except for the main board at which The McCarthy and his lady presided. For all, in the sight of their Lord, were equal; household servants and those who tilled the land, nursemaids and guests from nearby dwellings, all were part of the extended family or clan and were therefore entitled to join in the festivities. In this respect the Irish chieftains, royalty and rulers conducted themselves in a far different manner from that of the royals in other European countries of the time.

"An' what gown will ye choose for this evenin', Sheila, *aroon*?" asked Cait, the young woman who waited on her.

Three pretty gowns lay across her bed awaiting her decision.

"I think the blue velvet will be nice," Sheila replied. "I particularly like the lace collar and the way the sleeves are cut."

"Let me comb your hair, the way the grand ladies do," Cait coaxed.

"I want to wear the golden *torc* father gave me for my birthday," Sheila answered.

The celebrations lasted well into the wee hours of the morning. A sumptuous meal with platters of roast beef, lamb, pork and fresh salmon accompanied by a variety of vegetables was served by the *giolli*. Irish mead as well as Spanish wines in crystal decanters and pewter tankards were within easy reach of the many guests. And to further tempt satiated appetites, the sideboards flanking the walls displayed delicacies only the stouthearted could refuse — pies, jellies, pastries, trifles, puddings and tarts.

And as the turf was piled high in the great hearth, the bard, O'Faolán, ran his fingers across his harp. A hush came over the crowd, reverent silence as they eagerly awaited the musician's tales of valour and noble deeds.

The great wolf-hounds arose from their places in front of the fire, shook themselves, yawned and lay down again closer to the leaping flames. Sheila stretched forth her hand to stroke her favourite hound, Finn. She herself was seated on a stool close to the bard, her own harp within easy reach. For she knew that as soon as O'Faolán had rendered an account of the most recent victories and proclaimed the many heroic deeds wrought in battle by the McCarthy and his followers, her father having acknowl-edged the acclaim of all present would call upon her to perform.

She eagerly awaited the moment when the applause would die down and her handsome father would rise to his feet. Graciously thanking O'Faolán for his poem, his song of affection and praise, The McCarthy would then turn to his warriors. These men were faithful followers of the McCarthys, who from generation to generation had fought by the side of their leaders and counted it an honour. And then Sheila's moment would come. Knowing full-well where she was sitting, her father would fain ignorance and searching among the crowd, till all eyes followed his, he would seek her out.

"Ah! There you are, *mo stóirín.* Dear friends, tonight we have a rare treat."

She was awakened from her dream world as it coincided with reality. She saw the pride in his eyes as he gestured in her direction.

"My darling daughter, Sheila, pride of my heart, will honour us with a rendition of one of her favourite tunes. You be the judge if hers is not the loveliest voice in all Ireland."

The McCarthy took his place again and Sheila aided by O'Faolán mounted the dais and seated herself on a stool not too far from where her father and mother sat.

The applause was loud and long and when finally it died down, Sheila without hesitation got to her feet and addressed the guests.

"Thank you, thank you, one and all. My father is wont to exaggerate at times." She smiled at her father, then turned again to face her audience.

"It gives me great pleasure to sing for you a tune loved and known by everyone - The Coulin:

O lov'd maid of Broka, each fair one excelling!
The blush on thy cheek shames the apple's soft bloom,
More sweet than the rose-buds that deck thy lov'd
dwelling,
Thy lips shame their beauties, thy breath their perfume.

Come, bird of the evening, sweet thrush, void of sorrow,
Come greet her approach to thy flower-scented thorn,
And teach her fond warbler, thy lov'd notes to borrow,
To banish her coldness and soften her scorn.

O perch'd on thy green bough, each lov'd note
delighting,
How blest, happy bird! could I change lots with thee!
But, alas! while fast fetter'd, each prospect is blighting,
I would rather than Ireland again I were free!

But, adieu! though my hopes, by thy coldness and
scorning,
Fall faded like blossoms half brown on the tree,
May love bless your eve, though it blighted my morning,
I would rather than Ireland once more I were free!" [1]

---

[1]   From a literal translation of the original Irish, by
Hector MacNeill, Esq.

Chapter 2

"Slavery is a system of the most complete injustice."
- *Plato*

They sat on a rock near the lapping waters. Manacled in pairs – a sorry sight. They waited with bowed heads; the moisture from the salt sea and the misty hills behind them mixed with their salty tears. Beyond the rocky promontory, a ship, its sails furled, lay tossing gently on the incoming tide. Three small boats crammed with shivering, scantily clad youth were making ready to carry their cargoes to the waiting vessel, *The Jane,* while rough sailors shouted orders and the Sassenach (English) soldiers, swords at the ready, guarded those destined for deportation. Around this group of about fifty captives, the sullen silence of despair settled.

They had been rounded up from the surrounding counties by 'man-catchers' - agents of the government who were mounted and armed, carrying long whips with which to herd their miserable captives like cattle into holding-pens. Under these intolerable conditions, they were branded with the initials of the ship that would transport them to the West Indies or Virginia.

During their march to the seaport town of Kinsale, they were given only enough food to sustain life. If unable to support the journey, they were allowed to die by the wayside.

At this time there was a special demand for young women of childbearing age. As Henry Cromwell put it, the masters, or owners, as well as the white overseers "had only Negresses and Maroon women to solace them…" The man-catchers were paid £4 or £4.10 by the ships' captains for every young woman or child.

But since the loss of about one-fifth of those taken aboard was inevitable, for they frequently succumbed to disease, malnutrition and the rigours of the voyage, it was considered reasonable and nay necessary to cram as many human beings as possible into the holds of the slave ships.

Crouched round a bare hearth in
hard, frosty weather,
Three lonely helpless weans cling
Close together;
Tangled – those gold locks, once bonnie and bright –
There's no one to fondle the baby tonight.

"My mammie I want; Oh! My mammie
I want!"
The big tears stream down with the low wailing
chant.
Sweet Eily's slight arms enfold the gold
head:
"Poor weeny Willie, sure Mammie is
dead – "

– W. B. Yeats.

These words of W. B. Yeats could well describe the family and household of Sheila McCarthy.

In the twelfth century, a castle was built by the O'Flynn clan at Achad Dorbchon – Macroom in the Muskerry region.

By the mid-thirteenth century, The McCarthy became the dominant and most powerful family in that region.

References to Macroom reach back as far as 550 AD when the area was known as Achad Dorbchon and existed in the Kingdom of Muscraighe - Muskerry. Archaeological ruins, some still existing, include ring forts, stone forts, and *souterrains* - underground passageways. Large stones, some standing 15 feet tall and bearing Ogham inscriptions, dot the landscape.

The McCarthy family controlled about 232,300 acres of Muskerry land. By the 1600s, seven different members of the family had occupied the castle and held the position of Lord of Muskerry.

In the early hours of May 15, 1657, a sweaty and besmirched horseman rode into the castle *bawn*.[2] His feet scarce hit the ground when he shouted:

"The McCarthy! Take me to The McCarthy at once."

A *giolla*,[3] fetching water, heard his demand and dropping his bucket ran to the stranger.

"Come, come with me. The chieftain is within. I observed him not ten minutes hence."

The horseman was led into the great hall where he found the mighty McCarthy seated at table. He had just finished his morning victuals, a course oatmeal stirabout sweetened with honey and buttermilk.

Without formality, the horseman introduced himself as being of the Eóghan Core *sept*,[4] his name Mahon.

"*Céad mile fáilte*,"[5] McCarthy interrupted.

---

2   bawn – enclosed yard.

3   giolla – man-servant.

4   sept - clan

5   Céad mile fáilte – A hundred thousand welcomes

Then lowering his voice slightly, Mahon continued. "The 'Roundheads'[6] are fast advancing on Muskerry territory, m'Lord. I have ridden hard this night to bring ye word."

The McCarthy jumped up from his high-chair. "Sound the alarm," he bellowed to those close by. "See to the wee'ns," he spoke to a maid-servant, "and alert the Lady Sinead." He withdrew a gold piece from the pouch he wore over his dark kilt and approached Mahon.

"Take this, young Mahon, as a token of my sincere appreciation for yer loyalty this day. Now I'll not detain ye longer. Ye, no doubt, will wish to join yer own sept ere the Sassenach arrive."

"I'd deem it an honour great chief, were ye to permit me to join yer men."

McCarthy held out his arm.

"'A friend in need is a friend indeed.' I can always do with an extra fighting man."

Ere they left the hall, Mahon took note of its splendour as if to bear in mind forever what he knew in his heart would soon be an empty shell, a desolate burnt-out cavern. For who, regardless of his bravery, could stand against the mighty army the Puritan, Cromwell, had marshaled against them?

He marked well the huge fireplace of stone, the blazing hearth where the great wolf-hounds lay, the oak-panelled walls and ceiling; the heavy oak furniture, the crystal sconces, the silver plates scattered on tables and side-boards, and the thick carpets with their vivid Celtic patterns.

---

6   Roundheads – A member of England's Parliamentary party – 1642-1649: so called in contempt from their close - cropped hair.

"Aye, lad, 'tis a grand hall. One more reason not to allow the enemy to gain footing here." The McCarthy laid his hand on Mahon's shoulder and squeezed hard.

The day was fast dying when the Sassenach set up camp in the lush meadows within sight of the castle. They kept their fires burning far into the night and as McCarthy watched, he cursed the enemy loud and vehemently. He took comfort, however, from the thought that his wife and wee'ns were well on their way to the mountains and out of danger.

"We will make a stand. By God, we will! Mark your defenses," he cried to his men.

McCarthy's followers and household servants made hasty preparations for what they knew would be a fight to the death.

***

The first rays of a rising sun shone on the eastern horizon. It would be a clear day. Within the hour, the 'Roundheads' positioned themselves in easy reach of the castle walls. Swords drawn, they were ready to vent their spleen on the despised papist. But it was not their swords that caused The McCarthy and his men anguish, no indeed, the heart of the noble chief feared not the Sassenach's sword but the heavy loathsome guns that would soon breech those sturdy walls and against which he had no defense.

McCarthy knew full-well, like his countrymen in Drogheda, Wexford and every other town and village through which the Sassenach passed that not a member of his household would remain alive that day. In fact none in the territory of Muskerry would escape the vengeful atrocities of the Puritan. Urged on by their fanatical preachers who accompanied the army, the soldiers were ready for slaughter. Prayers such as the following spurred the 'Roundheads' to battle:

"I beg upon my hands and knees that the expedition against them (the Irish) be undertaken while the hearts and hands of our soldiery are hot; to whom, I will be bold to say, briefly: happy be he that shall reward them as they served us, and cursed be he who shall do the work of the Lord negligently. Cursed be he who holdeth back the sword from blood: yea cursed be he that maketh not the sword stark drunk with Irish blood..."

A Lamentation

There was lifted up one voice of woe,
One lament of more than mortal grief,
Through the wide South to and fro, for a
  fallen Chief.
In the dead of the night that cry thrilled
  through me,
I looked out upon the midnight air!
My own soul was all as gloomy,
  As I knelt in prayer...

From Loughmoe to yellow Dunanore
There was fear; the traders of Tralee
Gathered up their golden store,
  And prepared to flee;
For in ship and hall from night till morning,
Showed the first faint beamings of the sun,
All the foreigners heard the warning
  Of the Dreaded one!

"This," they spake, "portendeth death to us,
If we fly not swiftly from our fate!"
Self-conceited idiots! thus
    Ravingly to prate!
Not for base-born haggling Saxon trucksters.
Ring laments like those by shore and sea!
Not for churls with souls like hucksters
    Wailed the Banshee!

For the high Milesian race alone
Ever flows the music of her woe!
For slain heir to bygone throne,
    And for Chief laid low!
Hark!... again, methinks, I hear her weeping
Yonder! Is shee near me now, as then?
Or was but the night-wind sweeping
    Down the hollow glen?[7]

           - *Clarence Mangan*

Few there were who escaped the wrath of Cromwell's army as night closed over the desolate countryside. Among those who did manage to avoid the sword were eight young boys and four girls between the ages of twelve and fourteen. The soldiers in their zeal for blood, after destroying the castle and all its inhabitants, tracked the women and children into the hills. Ever mindful of the words of Cromwell's loyal representative then in charge in Ireland, Sir Charles Cooth:

---

7   This poem written to commemorate the death of Maurice Fitzgerald, Lord of Kerry, could well have been penned to honor The McCarthy.

"Kill the nits and you will have no lice," the soldiers were thorough in fulfilling their mission of murder, plunder and destruction that fateful evening.

Having dispatched the women and smaller children, an enterprising young sergeant halted the massacre of the youth. Realizing that a fair price was to be had for white slaves of a tender age, he had them bound and eventually marched to Kinsale harbour, there to await the next vessel sailing for the West Indies.

Among those captured was the beautiful young daughter of The McCarthy, Sheila, who was only twelve. Tall and slender for her age, she had long flowing hair the colour of ripe corn. "Blue were her eyes as the fairy flax"[8] and her milk-white skin was clear as the dawning day. Her rosebud mouth revealed pearly teeth when she smiled. A beauty, no doubt, she would be one day in the not too distant future.

As tears fell silently from her downcast eyes, her manacled companion, a girl older in years and experience and of a more robust constitution, tried to solace her grief.

"Don't be making yerself sick, *alanah*. God alone knows where we'll find ourselves and 'tis needin' all our strength we'll be to survive."

Sheila sighed, then lifted her head. She looked into the grey-blue eyes of the young woman to whom she was manacled: "Thank you for your kind words. I'm so frightened. What is to become of us, at all? If only my father would arrive in time to save us." The tears flowed again and with a great sob she uttered the words she scarce wanted to believe. "I fear he may be dead, even now. Killed by the sword of the Sassenach just as my mother was."

---

8   Longfellow, Henry Wadsworth, The Wreck of the Hesperus.

"I won't lie to you or pretend that there is any chance of your father rescuing us. The Sassenach don't leave anything alive, neither man nor beast. All is laid waste after them 'Roundheads' have captured a town or village," she whispered. "We have to face reality. We have no one to fend for us now. No one to care whether we live or die. We are alone. Only each other." The voice trailed off as the down-to-earth young woman at Sheila's side drew a little closer. "Tell me, *alanah*, what is your name? Mine is Ann, Ann Glover from Oranmore in the county of Galway. Some call me 'Goody', but it's only a sort of nickname."

"I'm Sheila McCarthy," answered the shy girl and she looked up into the kindly eyes of her companion.

"Then 'tis the daughter of The McCarthy you'll be?"

"Aye, I'm his oldest daughter."

Here she started to cry again. Great sobs which shook her delicate frame interrupted her words. "I saw them – kill my mother. She was minding the baby at the time. Poor little Liam, he didn't even cry. Then they killed my little sister, Maeve, as she ran away screaming." Again the tears flowed and she was unable to speak more.

Ann put her arm around her shoulder and gave her a hug, trying to reassure her. "Bad things are happening all over our country. So many good people lost." And she thought of her own parents who had been brutally stoned to death only a few days before. She wiped the tears from her own eyes with the back of her hand. "We have to live for them. We must live…" her words were interrupted.

"Get movin' you two," a soldier's voice rasped behind them.

The girls, holding on to each other, moved from the rock and joined several others heading toward the boats.

Just before they entered the skiffs, the soldiers removed the manacles and herded the unfortunate captives aboard. Sheila and Ann sat close to each other on the damp cold bottom of the boat, shivering, fearful.

As the sun was setting behind the western hills, they reached *The Jane* and were hurriedly taken on board.

This slave ship, like many others of its kind, was specially built for the African trade. It was fitted with shelves below deck thereby doubling the number of people it could carry. Only two feet of headroom was allowed, thus it was impossible to ever sit up. Captain Newton describes the conditions: "they were tightly packed in two rows one above the other, on each side of the ship, close to each other like books on a shelf. I have known them so close that the shelf would not easily contain one more….And I have known a man sent down among them to lay them in these rows to the greatest advantage, so that as little space as possible be lost."

On board ship, the slaves were again manacled two by two at the ankles. One can only imagine the shame and extreme difficulties this caused when one or the other "needed to use the stinking buckets which were the only means of relieving the wants of nature." Again O'Callaghan adds: "he (the slave) had to drag his fellow slave with him."

Under these appalling conditions, some 60,000 to 100,000 men, women and youth were shipped to the West Indies, chiefly Barbados, Montserrat and St. Kitts. Some were also transported to the plantations of colonial Virginia. The exact number will never be known for none ever returned to Ireland to tell their sorrowful stories.

"Mother o'God, have pity on us," a woman prayed as she watched in anguish as several young girls clinging to each other wept bitterly. "What in God's name can I do at all, at all to help them? What will become of them?"

After several hours the crying subsided as worn out and hungry bodies drifted into uneasy sleep.

The ship was underway and would not stop again until it reached the Cape Verdes Islands.

Many aboard that evening would not live to see those islands where the vessel was scheduled to anchor for three or four days to take on supplies. This stay only added to the discomfort of the pitiful captives, who were "confined to the hold with the hatches secured to prevent any attempt of escape or mutiny." In a semi-tropical climate, existence becomes intolerable. O'Callaghan continues, "they were fed by buckets of sloppy food being lowered down to them!"

"We're being treated like pigs," Ann whispered.

"I can't eat that awful mess," Sheila answered.

"You'll have to eat, horrid though it is, *alanah*, otherwise you'll go the way of the O'Maras," she said, referring to the burial at sea a few days before.

What was written by a Clare-man some two hundred years later can well apply to the conditions on board *The Jane*.

> Without a prayer or passing bell,
> The shroudless armies hourly smell,
>   Miserere!
> The dying, ghastlier than the dead;
> With blanched lips have vainly said,
> 'Give us this day our daily bread.'
>   Parce nobis Domine!

It was estimated that the loss from each ship was about 20 percent and this, in time, amounted to at least 10,000 deaths as a result of disease, malnutrition and the horrific conditions under which the slaves were transported. But the English Captain of *The Jane* had calculated well. An Irish white slave had cost him £4.10. In the island he would receive between £10 and £35, giving him a nice profit of about £5000 and all accomplished within the time frame of nine to twelve weeks. A goodly sum, this was far more lucrative than the African trade.

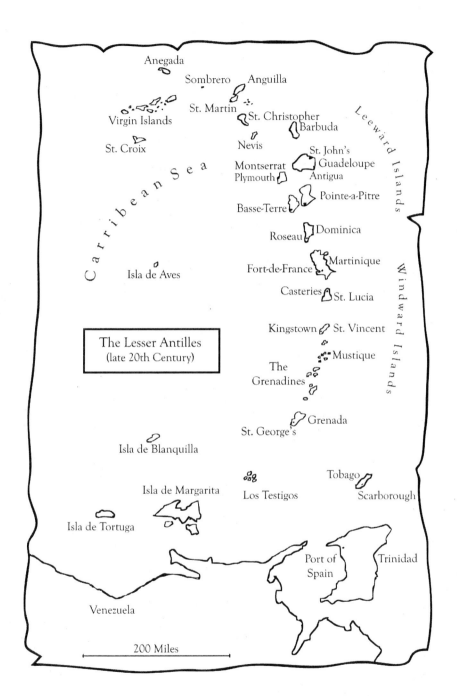

The Lesser Antilles
(late 20th Century)

Chapter 3

"Slavery is a system contrary to the fundamental law of all societies."

- *Montesquieu*

Conditions aboard *The Jane* were past enduring. Herded together in the belly of the ship the men and women were separated, the men placed in the forepart beyond the main mast, and the women and children towards the stern, with a strong barrier between them. They were treated more like cattle than human beings.

Poor ventilation made it impossible to escape the foul air – odors from stale vomit, unwashed bodies and the stench from the crude bucket set in a corner to collect human waste. In addition almost all the captives were sea-sick within a few days of setting out to sea. And as a consequence of eating or trying to eat food contaminated with feces, dysentery or the 'bloody flux' soon became an ever present scourge on board.

They were forced to eat to keep them alive – stale biscuits and greasy cabbage soup, for the pork with which the cabbage was boiled had been removed.

A flimsy partition separated the young girls, Ann and Sheila, from the Fitzwilliam family. James and his wife were both in their seventies, but Cromwell's soldiers cared little for that fact. What earthly use these old people would have been on a tobacco plantation is difficult to fathom. Accompanying them, at least initially, were their two sons and daughter – a most gracious lady who was attended by a maidservant. The sons and the father had been forced to leave the women-folk to join the rest of the male slaves in the other end of the vessel. These gentle folk endured the same indignities and hardships as the younger more robust captives, but unlike the young folk they soon succumbed to the rigors of the journey. After four weeks at sea, the bodies of James and Cornelia Fitzwilliam were dumped overboard.

The loss of two captives at first caused some concern to the Captain. But since these two were old and would scarce have fetched a decent price, he did not give the matter a great deal of thought other than to order that an extra ladle of victuals be given the slaves.

"Increase the soup portions," he shouted to the cook. "This lot's hardly worth shippin', puny all of 'em, needin' cuddlin' ere they succumb to the vapours!"

Ann dipped the end of her skirt into a tin cup. She had saved a little water from the noonday serving. Gently, she wiped the fevered brow and tried to cool the parched lips of her friend.

"Come on now, *alanah*. You must fight this sickness," she whispered in Sheila's ear.

Sheila moaned and slowly opened her bloodshot eyes. She tried to answer but not a sound could she make. Only her sad frightened gaze told Ann her real feelings and condition.

Beside herself, Ann was determined, come what may, that she would not be parted from her 'charge.' For that was how she considered their relationship from the moment they were shacked together on the dock site in Kinsale.

For the next few days, Ann fought incessantly for the life which had become more precious than her own, sacrificing the paltry portion of water that was hers and patiently forcing it drop by drop onto the burning tongue and down the swollen throat until finally the fever broke.

In the Gaelic tongue, remembering a poem from the past, she gently rocked the frail body and recited the soothing words:

> Sleep, my child! For the rustling trees,
> Stirred by the breath of summer breeze,
> And fairy songs of sweetest note,
> Around us gently float.

> Sleep! For the weeping flowers have shed
> Their fragrant tears upon thy head,
> The voice of love hath sooth'd thy rest,
> And thy pillow is a mother's breast.
> > Sleep, my child!

> Weary hath pass'd the time forlorn,
> Since to your mansion I was borne,
> Tho' bright the feast its airy halls,
> And the voice of mirth resounds from its
> > walls.
> > Sleep, my child!

> Sleep, my child! For the rustling trees,
> Stirr'd by the breath of summer breeze,
> And fairy songs of sweetest note,
> Around us gently float.[9]

---

9   Cusheen Loo – Translated from the Irish by J.J. Callanan, Irish poet (1795-1824). Not all the verses are quoted here.

With each new day, it seemed, new hardships had to be overcome. As the ship drew closer to the tropics, the overwhelming heat and the accumulation and multiplication of lice and fleas added further discomfort. Once healthy and vibrant bodies were drained of all their vitality.

Those taken with fever suffered most from the stifling heat. One of those who witnessed Sheila's distress and who was fortunate to escape declared years later: "The closeness of the place and the unaccustomed heat, added to the number in the ship, which was so crowded that each had scarcely room to turn himself, almost suffocated us."

This overwhelming heat, particularly so for Irish captives used to cool weather and fresh air, produced copious amounts of perspiration, so much so that the air became unfit for respiration. A variety of other smells vile and loathsome brought on a sickness from which many of the slaves died. These wretched conditions were further aggravated by the chafing of the chains which by this time had become insupportable.

Ann looked around as a shaft of light brought the morning. Several had died during the night. They lay shackled to the living. It was a scene of horror which in her mind conjured up thoughts of Hell. She heard the groans of the dying and the shrieks of women heavy with child. Young children half-starved whimpered and looked wide-eyed in vain at helpless mothers.

"Oh dear God," she prayed, "deliver us from this evil."

After about eight days, swollen and cramped limbs were in danger of further complications. Hence, the slaves were ordered to mount the ladder onto the deck. They came slowly; several so weak that excrement ran down their legs.

Humiliated and embarrassed, tears of shame spilling from blood-shot eyes, many women gave up the effort and simply collapsed before they reached the ladder.

Once on deck those of sturdier nature were commanded to sing and dance to the tunes rendered by a fiddler or bagpiper.

Pitiful indeed was the sight – stumbling, exhausted, pale-faced, these miserable human beings were scarcely able to use their feet. Yet, they were forced to do so under the threat of the whip.

It was hot, sultry. The afternoon saw little or no headway as the vessel lay in a lazy stupor. With not the slightest whiff to ruffle the sails, the sailors were in need of some diversion. Captain Wallace ordered the first mate to bring 'the girls' on deck.

Several young women, some as young as ten years were hustled onto the deck. At first the bright sunlight was blinding. They stumbled and clung to each other. Then they were herded to an open space behind the main mast.

"Undress!" the order was harsh.

The women looked at each other. Did they hear right? There were several sailors in plain view, gawking.

"Undress, wash and be quick about it."

As the women still hesitated, the swift swish of a leather lash was heard.

Eventually, the older women devised a plan. They formed a circle around the tubs of water as the younger girls undressed and washed. Then, they in turn did likewise for the older women. It was a relief to feel the coolness of the salt water. But if they thought their captors had wished to show some compassion in allowing them to bathe, they were very soon awakened to reality.

The orgies which ensued were thankfully not witnessed by Ann and Sheila. Both had been too weak to mount the ladder. The cries, piercing, chilling, agonizing echoed and re-echoed below deck. In vain did they try to block the sounds, stopping their ears, wrapping long woolen shawls about their heads.

***

Four weeks had passed. *The Jane* was making headway slowly but surely towards the Cape Verde Islands. A stopping-off place for many transatlantic vessels, these rugged volcanic outcroppings serviced slave ships as well as trading vessels.

In the early morning hours, *The Jane* dropped anchor in the calm waters of Mindelo on São Vicente. Towards mid-day, the hatches were thrown open. Cries of "water, water," ascended on the foul air. For the past week, the water supply had been severely curtailed. Less than two pints a day, barely enough to sustain the captives, was the norm. Dehydration had plagued the entire vessel for well over a week, resulting in bouts of vomiting and diarrhea and several deaths. As the dehydration spread among the captives, each afflicted person experienced rapid weight loss, fatigue, and an overpowering listlessness. Tongues started to swell, making swallowing impossible, and the eyes sank back into the head. Finally, those who suffered the most experienced a dream-like state, which usually preceded heart failure.

Several women and children were lost in this manner; their bodies then simply dumped overboard.

The ship weighed anchor in Bridgetown, Barbados on the last day of May, in 1657.

The owners of plantations on the island had grown rich over the years, many converting their chief crops from tobacco to sugar cane. These holdings were owned by men whose names were mostly British - Newton, Skeete, Waldon and others - gentry for the most part who wished to retire to a more leisurely lifestyle. They held seats in the island Council and Assembly. Their homes were spacious and particularly well fortified, for there was always the threat of slave uprisings. The governor at this time was Lord Willoughby.

An idle lot, for the most part, the landowners lived like lords. Eating off gold plates and dressing in the latest London fashion, they were waited upon by bewigged butlers, pages, coachmen, while the modest parts of the mansions thronged with a retinue of cooks, washers, maids, stable-boys, and table-attendants. They over-ate and over-drank and spent much of their time horseracing, gambling and wenching.

****

It was a very hot day. The seas were calm. A heaviness seemed to hang over the island. Not a whiff of air to cool burning cheeks.

The captives aboard *The Jane* were eager to be liberated from the inferno in which they had existed for over six weeks, ever since they left the Cape Verde Islands. Little did they know what conditions awaited them on the island of Barbados.

As one by one they came up on deck they were both confused and bewildered, having lived for many long weeks in a world of darkness, the bright sunlight was blinding. It took several moments for each slave to adjust to the glare. Some stumbled forward, others of a weaker nature fell. But the rough sailors had little patience; they too wished to go ashore, to partake of fresh victuals and enjoy a brief respite ere the cargo of sugar or tobacco for the return journey had to be loaded on board.

Once on deck, the slaves were severely restricted and the females were unable to communicate with any male member of their families. The men were ordered to one end of the vessel while the women were told to step behind a canvas curtain hung between two of the masts. There, they were ordered to take off their clothes and wash in the tubs already set up for that purpose.

Unaccustomed, even from childhood, to strip naked many protested. Then the voice of an older woman commanded silence.

"Sure, aren't we all women. Let's be thankful that the bloody captain had the presence of mind to give us some privacy." Then, beginning to undress, she continued, "I, for one, will be relieved to shake off some of these infernal vermin that have plagued me."

Following her example, the more mature among them slowly removed their garments and helped each other to bathe. The water was fresh, saved from the Cape Verdes, and was warmed by long exposure to the sun.

After their baths, the women sat on the deck drying their hair. All shades and colours, from yellow to sandy, brown flecked with gold, black as the raven's wings, and red as the Autumn leaves, the heavy tresses fell to their hips.

Their undergarments they also washed and set to dry in the tropical sun. With little or no shade, they soon felt the burning rays on their pale bodies. They could not long endure such exposure. Some were about to don skirts and bodices when the canvas curtain was drawn aside and the captain, carrying a stool, stepped inside.

A gasp arose. Some ran to the canvas turning their backs to the captain. Those standing immediately in front crouched and tried to hide their nakedness with their long hair. But the Captain had a job to do and he would not be deterred.

"You there," he pointed to the woman nearest to him. "Come here. I mean to get what is rightfully mine from you lot."

The woman hesitated.

"Do I have to get the whip?"

Slowly, the woman drew closer. The Captain stood up, grabbed her by the arm and held her firmly. Then he examined the muscles of arms and thighs. Her mouth was inspected. He asked her age. And so it was with each woman in turn. When he was satisfied, he ordered that they dress. Then calling for a sailor, he shouted, "Take this lot below. We'll unload in the morning."

After a night of fitful sleep, the captives were again brought on deck.

Below on the choppy waters, a boat manned by two sailors awaited. Then without further delay, the slaves were ordered to descend the sisal ladder one after another.

As soon as the boat was filled, they set off toward the shore.

Mindful that the 'goods' must not be damaged, they nevertheless hurried them out of the boat and into the knee-high waters, goading them toward the beach.

A pathetic sight, indeed, were the women, their long skirts wet through and through as they waded ashore and fell exhausted on the rocks.

The friends, Sheila and Ann, managed somehow to keep close to each other. No words passed between them but their thoughts were identical as they reached dry land and looked back across the clear blue waters in the direction from which they had come.

Ireland, how very far away it seemed now. Ireland, would they ever again see its lush green fields, its laughing streams, its flowery meadows? When would they hear again the warbling of the linnet or thrush, the bleating of newborn lambs? When might they feel the caress of dew-drenched mosses or smell perfumed cowslips as bare feet lightly skipped through the dell. Where was the cry of the curlew? Where the quiet of the misty hallows on a summer evening?

With heavy hearts they turned to face the unfamiliar land they would be forced to call home. The tall palm trees, seen for the first time, stood like sentinels, straight, slim, unbending. Even their crowns of stilted leaves studded with clusters of brown hairy balls, curious and ugly to their straining eyes, were foreboding.

With unsteady feet they climbed the dusty trail leading from the beach to higher ground. Upon reaching the top, a vast expanse of cultivated land spread out before them. It seemed to touch the horizon. As far as the eye could see, a large plant with broad sticky leaves and tubular flowers was the only crop visible.

Bent backs and bowed heads were raised as the newcomers came into view.

"Ah!" It was a fearsome cry. But barely audible. Sheila's eyes, however told more as she looked away from

Landing on Barbados

the strangers to her friend Ann. Then finding her tongue,
"Look, look, what kind of people are they?" she asked.

Ann was unable to answer. She stood a moment, gazing,
bewildered. For the first time in their lives they beheld men
and women of colour, black and brown, then miserable

whites, red ones with puffy lips, blocked faces, ugly to behold. Their hands and legs red, raw and bleeding.

"Get a move on. No time for day-dreaming. You'll be joinin' 'em ere long, I'll wager," a sailor admonished.

Although the dry land was once more beneath their feet and they were no longer subjected to the rolling and swaying of *The Jane,* they stumbled and even fell as they were roughly herded down the street of this foreign new environment. Buildings were made of brick and reached two or more stories. White men, haughty and overbearing rode on horseback or in carriages. The newcomers saw no more as they were shoved into a warehouse – a large makeshift shelter hastily thrown together overnight for this particular batch of slaves. They had been kept for two days and two nights on board ship since the docking.

Now for the first time in over two months, the men, women and youth were all assembled in the same place. Hopes ran high that this occurrence might enable them to be reunited as families once more.

For the next few days they remained huddled together wherever they found a little space. No amenities were provided but they were given extra food and water. On the third day they were washed down with seawater and deloused, provided with a clean shift and led in groups or individually to the auction area.

As soon as the prospective buyers had assembled, the auction began.

The young men were the first to be paraded before the landowners. Their future masters walked among them, checking frame, muscle and even teeth.

Four young men mounted the platform. Among those awaiting their turn was a tall, well-built youth of about eighteen. His name was Rory O'Connor. He had a head of thick wavy dark brown hair, a fair complexion and usually a ready smile. Rory was a man to make the best of most unpleasant situations, but this unnatural barbarous and incomprehensible affair so completely alien to anything he had ever seen in his life caused his blood to boil. It was with extreme control that he forced himself to remain in his place. He wanted desperately to jump upon the platform in front of the auctioneer and tear him and the 'mighty' plantation owners to pieces.

"Open yer mouth," he heard the order to another slave. "One, two, three teeth missing. That will be ten shillings less. This slave is worth no more than £20," the buyer declared.

Rory's turn came. He mounted the platform, then hesitated. The rough hand of the over-seer pushed him forward: "No insolence from you, bucko," he threatened, "or 'tis the lash that fine broad back will feel, I guarantee."

Rory's pride was hurt but the crude insensitive examinations his person now underwent aroused his deepest resentment. He would remember! A day would come when this incident and many others that he foresaw would be his lot would demand justice.

Sheila and Ann watched from a distance. They glanced at each other but made no comment.

The slaves were divided into two classes – those who would work in the fields and those, of a more refined nature, who would work in the house. These categories were further broken into groups of both black and white field slaves according to age and strength, each with a specific job.

The first group consisted of the strongest most mature black and white men and women for the actual field operations. These would perform the hardest work on the plantations and were called the 'great gang.' During crop planting time which started in February and continued into early May many more hours of continuous labour were required than at any other time of the year. The 'great gang' was again divided into smaller groups allowing two shifts of twelve hours each thus providing for a twenty-four hour workday. Driven by whips they were not allowed a mid-morning break but instead received extra food and an hour to eat at dinnertime.

Gang number two, called the 'little gang,' was made up of adolescents, the average age being about fifteen. These slaves weeded the fields and planted most of the food crops, corn, manioc, etc.

Children ages five or six up to eleven or twelve formed the third gang. These little ones were called the 'meat pickers' or sometimes the 'hog minders,' as this name implied their main job was to collect grass or fodder for the animals. They also attended to the fowl and other small animals and made up about fifteen percent of the total slave population.

A fourth gang, an elite group of skilled workers, were employed as carpenters, masons, coopers, potters, etc.

The business of the auction continued. Soon it was time for the women to be brought forward. They were pushed onto the platform. The older women were auctioned off first having been stripped naked, prodded and poked, measured and examined.

However, it was the younger ones who were thoroughly scrutinized, for many of them would be used as concubines or sexual objects by their English masters. In this instance, the buyer often went to the expense of having a 'churgeon' or midwife to assure himself that the young woman he was about to purchase was indeed a virgin.

The small children were the last to be purchased. Amid tears and cries of terror, they were eventually separated from all they had known and loved and turned over to the care of an overseer who would train them as pages or housemaids. Unfortunately, many were also used for more 'sinister reasons.'

Sheila was mortified when her turn came to be squeezed and prodded. Tears of shame and anger coursed down her flushed cheeks as she stood before the haughty 'gentleman.' Her head bowed, she could not look at him. Nor did she cease weeping till well into the night when from sheer exhaustion, she finally fell asleep on the damp ground under a mango tree.

The following morning, the slaves were awakened at sun-up. Sheila had one moment of joy that day when she saw her friend, Ann, lying only a few feet away.

"Where are we?" she asked, puzzled, looking around.

"On the Spencer plantation, *alanah*."

Still dazed, Sheila had no recollection of the happenings of the day before. How she had arrived at the plantation; the horrible, debasing, embarrassing moments when she stood naked during the auction; the long dusty walk later to the plantation; nor the downpour that soaked her to the skin as she neared her journey's end.

She was given a calabash of water and a hunk of coarse bread for breakfast. These were handed to her by a tall African woman. She was none too friendly and spoke words most of the newcomers didn't understand. After several futile attempts to explain herself, the African woman called Hailey turned to an older white slave for help. Burnt and blistered from long hours in the hot sun, Maggie looked and acted much older than her thirty-five years. Later, Sheila learned that Maggie had been working for nigh on eight years at the Spencer plantation. She had not always worked in the fields. At first she had been assigned to clean the vegetables and do other menial tasks in the 'big house.' But after she had a fight with the head cook, she was banished from the kitchen and sent into the fields. She had come, initially, as an indentured servant and should have had her freedom a year before but because of her behaviour, she was told she had forfeited that privilege.

"Ya' all start work, at once," she declared. And then she proceeded to assign a task to each slave according to the directions given her.

"You, dae, she pointed at Sheila, "You go to dee 'big house' and you," she signed to Anne, "you go in dee fields."

The friends parted. Anne followed the Negro slaves into a tobacco field while Sheila made her way, head held high despite her fear and anguish, to the Spencer mansion.

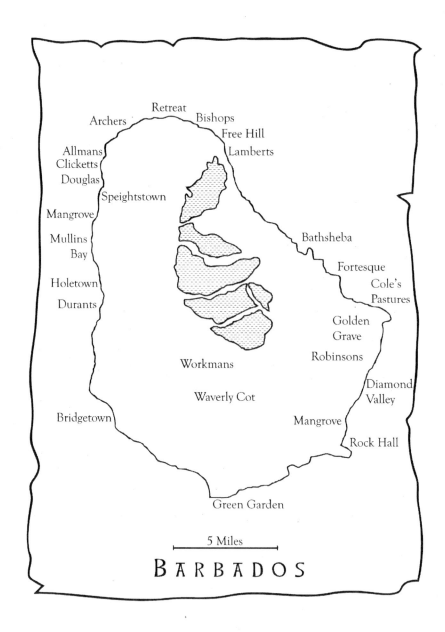

Retreat
Bishops
Archers
Free Hill
Lamberts
Allmans
Clicketts
Douglas
Speightstown
Mangrove
Mullins
Bay
Holetown
Durants
Bathsheba
Fortesque
Cole's
Pastures
Golden
Grave
Robinsons
Workmans
Diamond
Valley
Waverly Cot
Bridgetown
Mangrove
Rock Hall
Green Garden

5 Miles

BARBADOS

Chapter 4

"Corrupted freemen are the worst of slaves."
                                    - *Garrick*

The Spencer mansion was protected on one side by a grove of mango trees and on the other by coconut palms. A carriageway of about half a mile led from the main entrance to the rutted roadway, while the cultivated fields of the tobacco plantation spread out from behind the house as far as the eye could see.

Spencer, an English Protestant of the Puritan persuasion, had come to the island some ten years before with many others of his class. He had been given lands in the county of Cork, Ireland while still a very young man. But wishing to further his holdings and increase his fortune, he, with the blessing of the Earl of Carlisle, undertook a voyage to Barbados.

There, through the intercession of the same protectorate, he was granted considerable lands with the stipulation they be used to raise tobacco plants and if possible sugar cane. These commodities would be shipped directly to England. Upon the receipt of the products of his land, Spencer would receive in return a boatload of Irish slaves. The agreement stated that: "Slaves, primarily females and children of both sexes would await transportation from the harbour of Kinsale, Ireland."

The detailed truth about Charles Edwin Spencer has quite another tone. He had incurred considerable debts through gambling and other 'hushed up' indiscretions. The Earl of Carlisle, whose niece Spencer had married, offered

Charles 8,000 acres of some of the best land on the island of Barbados provided that he leave Ireland immediately. It was also stipulated that his wife and child would follow in due course. The latter part of the arrangement would not be realized.

Spencer was a bully, a drunkard and a womanizer. In the ten years he had spent on the island, he did little to protect the white slaves from their cruel and unprincipled over-seers, many of whom were black. He had no love for the Irish Catholics or anyone related to them. 'Were they not heathen and barbarian?' Uncouth, they were in his mind ignorant, lazy and undisciplined. Speaking a barbarian tongue, they seemed incapable of learning the 'refinements' of the Saxon language.

It mattered little - the next cargo of tobacco bound for the fatherland would replenish the supply on the return journey. No one would even know or care how many unfortunate women and children were forced to labour in the tobacco and sugar cane fields of Barbados and the other West Indian islands.

****

Sheila was conducted to the back of the house. A rather stout black woman named Hannah was in charge of the kitchen and the many pantries adjoining it.

When she saw Sheila, she put her hands on her hips, pursed her lips and opened her eyes wide, looking her up and down. She asked herself what kind of creature she was now beholding. Was she human and not just a figment of her imagination? To be sure she had seen white girls before – in the fields there were hundreds of them. But this child – frail, delicate, skin clearer than the whitecaps on a stormy sea, could not be human. Perhaps, yes perhaps, she could be one of those other world creatures the Irish slaves spoke about sometimes. She thought a moment. "Yes, *síog*[10], that was it!" she exclaimed.

Sheila, surprised by the Gaelic word, was about to speak when Hanna interrupted, "What on earth will you be able to do?"

Meantime, there were vegetables, lots of them to prepare. Guests were expected later in the day and she didn't have time to waste on newcomers.

Hannah gestured as she again spoke, "Ain't goin' te git much of an 'tin' out of ya, I reckon. Never did see the likes afore." Then she raised her voice and called, "Nitty, come here."

Immediately a young black girl, a little older than Sheila, came from one of the pantries. Her hands were wet.

"Take this one with ya and learn her good. Ya hear?" Hannah ordered.

"Yes'm," Netty answered, and led the way to the pantry from which she had come.

Inside the windowless room there was a table and a tub of water, otherwise it was bare of all furniture.

The table held what Sheila surmised were fruits or vegetables; she wasn't sure which, never having seen such strange food before. Soon she would learn that yams, corn, eggplants and manioc were considered vegetables while mangoes, oranges, bananas and guavas were fruit.

Handing her a crude blade, Netty said: "Ya clean and cut these for cookin'." She placed several yams in front of Sheila. Then to show her own importance and authority, she added: "An' be quick. We ain't got all day."

---

10   síog – fairy

Although Sheila knew some words in the tongue of the Sassenach, she was unable to speak the English language. On this occasion, however she understood what was expected of her.

Sheila held her head high and hid the pain in her heart. She, the daughter of The McCarthy was relegated to the status of a lowly slave, fit for nothing better than peeling vegetables.

Although at the time she was humiliated and felt abandoned, she thanked God for her lowly indoor position upon seeing the other white women and children come in from the fields at the end of the day. She could scarcely believe their pitiful condition. Those who had accompanied her on board *The Jane,* among them her friend Ann, were almost unrecognizable. Blistered, swollen faces, swollen cut and bleeding hands and feet, legs and arms so burned it was plain to see why the black slaves called them 'Redshanks.'

After they had hastily eaten a frugal meal of manioc and fish served in a calabash, the newly arrived slaves were required to build a simple shelter from the bits and pieces of sticks and leaves they could salvage in the area. Four or six forks stuck into the ground to support the sidewalls of reeds and a roof of palms or banana leaves were all they could count on.

For several hours by the light of a tropical moon, the newcomers worked on their individual sleeping quarters. Finally, exhausted, they lay on the bare ground and fell into fitful sleep.

Unlike her friend Ann, Sheila returned to the Manor after her evening meal and slept on the earthen floor in the same windowless annex which housed the vegetables and where she had spent her entire day. In the darkness, she was free to give vent to her pent-up grief and loneliness. Netty had quickly succumbed to sleep and lay a few feet away in a fetal position. She would not hear the heart-breaking sobs. She would not see the tears that welled up in those beautiful blue eyes and course down the tired face of the little Irish girl. Only the cockroaches and the centipedes, the night breezes sighing in the cracks and crevices witnessed her sorrow.

And the fitful sleepless nights brought only vivid pictures of her homeland and the loved ones of her happy childhood.

> I dream of a land beyond the sea,
> I dream of my home, where I long to be.
>> I see once again the verdant dale,
>> The tree clad mountains and the flowery

vale.

> I dream of a castle proud and strong,
> I dream of that fortress that's stood so long.
>> I see there, my father handsome and brave,
>> And my mother weeping beside a grave.

> I dream of the days, happy days so free,
> And I long for the way that used to be,
>> And I pray to my God who dwells above,
>> To bless and protect the land I love.

The following morning at 6:00 am, as the sun appeared on the horizon, all the slaves were awakened. A meager breakfast of coarse hard cassava bread and a calabash of water was their fare before they were herded into the sugar and tobacco fields once more. Nor would they leave those sun-drenched fields till sun-down, during which time the newcomers were allowed only one half-hour break in which to eat a midday meal of cold fish and the island's staple food, cassava.

Although each day brought with it a continuous round of work, toiling in the fields from early morning until a few moments before darkness fell, the period from February to May – the harvest time for sugar cane - was the busiest of the year. During these months, the work lasted far into the night. It was backbreaking toil. Machetes were used to cut the cane. Considerable skill was required of those who performed this work. The stalks had to be cut low on the stems which were very tough, while care had to be taken not to damage the bud from which the new shoots would spring the next year.

When the canes were cut, they were loaded onto a cart drawn by slaves or donkeys and taken to the sugar mill – a structure erected in the middle of the cane field. Those who worked at the mill had to be strong and skillful. The hours were long, longer than required by the other 'gangs' or the newcomers, at this point in time. The work with the canes continued day and night as the boiling vats had to be maintained at a certain temperature and constantly fed with juice. This juice was extracted by crushing the canes, which was then taken to the copper vats and kept at a constant boil. Because of their efforts and the continual and exhausting workload, the white men who attended these vats were very soon worn out and quickly succumbed not only to pulmonary diseases but to many of the tropical maladies as well. The death toll among them was particularly high.

After a few days of boiling the sugar, crystals formed. A wet clay was then placed on the mixture, which helped to separate the crystals from the molasses. After that, the vats were taken to the cooling house where the sugar was then bagged and made ready for shipment to England.

The harvest time was the busiest on the plantations, but even more physically exhausting for the majority of the slaves was when the land had to be prepared for planting. No ploughs were available on the Spencer plantation; hence all the hard work of digging had to be done with a hoe: a most arduous task, indeed, involving as it did, in the case of the sugar cane, the making of holes ten inches deep and two feet apart. November was planting time. It took almost sixteen months for the crop to be mature. That is of course if the weather cooperated.

The West Indies is an area plagued by hurricanes. For the sugar cane plantations of Barbados and the other islands this was often disastrous.

Chapter 5

"Slavery is a system of outrage and robbery."
                                        -Socrates

It had been almost three months to the day when Sheila and her enslaved countrymen, women, and children, had landed on the island of Barbados.

The shades of night had not yet been drawn from across the morning sky when the wake-up call sounded – the blast of a horn, shrill, piercing. Groggy, not fully awake, many murmured.

"It's earlier than usual! What's the reason?" a young woman inquired.

Those familiar with such matters held their tongues. An eerie, tense atmosphere pervaded the compound. Only the wind made noises. It came in gusts irritable, erratic, forceful. Bleary-eyed, many of the slaves stumbled trying to find their way in the dark.

Within ten minutes of the wake-up call, the voice of the head overseer sounded harsh and angry, "Ye all ha' been awoke this mornin' to bear witness to what's in store fer anyone of ye who dares to disobey orders. It matters not if the slave be man, woman, or child. His fate will be the same."

It must be remembered that the Irish, as a whole, did not speak the English language. The words of the overseer fell mostly on deaf ears. Confused and bewildered in a strange new world, they were severely handicapped. Only those of the hardiest stock would survive the backbreaking toil of the fields. Those who had education – the privileged families who had knowledge of the English language, and who were therefore assigned to work in the Big House – were spared the rigors of climate and hard labour for the most part. These lived their miserable lives as house servants and nursemaids.

A bloody sun broke through the waves on the eastern horizon. Then a gasp, as if from one voice, broke the stillness, as a shaft of crimson light slowly crept across the frightened faces of all present. Finally, the overseer and his shackled captive, a white male of about twenty-five years, were the focus of all eyes, as the blazing sun rose steadily out of the seas.

The young man, though of robust physique, was badly sunburned; his feet and hands scarred and blistered. He was pushed rather than led to the whipping post.

He held his head high and had a defiant attitude in spite of the fate that he knew awaited him. He would go to his death not as a lowly slave but as a Christian, a Catholic Christian following the example of his leader – Christ. This Sheila determined as her thoughts turned to prayers on behalf of the youth. It was a scene from the New Testament repeated. Here before her was the Christ on his journey to Golgotha.

The flogging post consisted of a single stake driven into the ground with a crossbar at the top. Upon reaching the spot, the clothes were ripped from the slave's body. His hands were tied to the crossbar in such fashion that the body was lifted off the earth leaving the toes just touching the ground. Then the overseer stood back, and having removed the whip from his belt, measured the distance from the victim and delivered the first blow. The next stroke criss-crossed the first and so it was repeated until the young man fainted. To bring him to, a bucket of salt water was thrown over him. Upon regaining consciousness, the flogging continued. But that was not the extent of the sufferings inflicted upon this heroic slave. Vinegar as well as pepper were rubbed into the open wounds now visible.

The flogging was the most savage thing Sheila had ever witnessed, the moans of the dying youth wrenching. The young girl trembled, felt limp and faint. She could not endure the sight any further. Averting her eyes, she turned her head and tried to block out the horror. But the sound of the lash allowed no reprieve for her tortured soul.

It was not until the victim had expired that the assembled slaves were allowed to partake of their morning repast and then hounded off to their daily tasks.

Unable to eat anything, Sheila tried to keep up with the other house slaves as they made their way back to attend to their respective chores.

****

"What is the hour?" a voice enquired without in the yard.

"It must be close to noon," came a reply. "At least my inners tell me so."

"But it's so dark!" Sheila interjected.

The half-light in which Sheila and her negro companions worked suddenly faded. It was almost pitch black. The two girls groped their way to the entrance of the shed.

Outside, a shaft of light from behind a threatening dark cloud gave a ghostly appearance to the yard and the slaves working there. The wind which had been blowing in strong gusts from the east since early morning had picked up considerably, preventing the slaves from doing meaningful work.

Unable to carry on in the fields, many slaves were fighting their way towards the shelter of sturdier buildings. Sheila and her companion crawled slowly towards the Big House. When they finally reached the back entrance, they found several other slaves huddled together close to the doorway outside. The air was thick with flying objects, and clouds of swirling vegetation.

Those who had experienced hurricanes in the past were well aware of the destruction and devastation caused by such storms. Wide-eyed with fear, Sheila and her companion made futile attempts to protect themselves as coconut trees came crashing down and blade-like palms cut deep gashes in unprotected skin.

They banged on the stout door and shuttered windows unsuccessfully for several minutes, their terrified voices lost in the howling wind. Then the door was flung open and almost as quickly slammed shut again by two burly negro men. It was just enough time for Sheila and Netty to gain entrance.

Once inside, they sank trembling to the wooden floor. Netty's teeth chattered. Sheila, wet with perspiration, and drained of all colour, whimpered: "Oh, God, deliver us from evil."

48

Those close-by, who understood the Irish tongue, answered, "Amen."

Very little light penetrated the shuttered windows. It took several minutes for Sheila to become accustomed to the darkness and even then she could only guess how many slaves and servants really occupied the room.

A few minutes later, Sheila realized that the person sitting beside her was an Irish lad. She couldn't be sure of his age, but she surmised from his voice and behaviour that he was seventeen or eighteen.

"Are you hurt?" he asked.

"No, not really. A few scratches. But I'm scared," Sheila answered, "This is the worst storm I've ever known in my whole life."

"It's called a hurricane. They plague these islands almost every year around these summer months."

"You've been here a long time, then?"

"Aye, too long. What's your name?"

"My name is Sheila."

"Ah! You're the *cailín bán* all the lads talk about![11] Then it's happy I am to meet you even under these miserable conditions. I'm Liam. Liam O'Reilly from County Clare."

The howling winds and the torrential rains that now accompanied them drowned out Sheila's response. But the confident voice beside her gave her courage.

A loud noise without, a rending and shattering sound, signaled to Sheila and Netty that the shed they called their 'home' had been ripped apart.

---

11   cailín bán – fair-haired girl, special, pretty

Sheila clung to the youth beside her. Her clammy hands gripped his arm. Her body was shivering, shivering with fear. She felt cold.

Like Sheila, others within the stuffy confines drew closer together. Netty abandoned her place and sought the protection of a large black man. Small children screamed, a woman cried out in terror. The men-folk cursed and swore under their breaths: they would find a way to escape the insufferable state in which they existed.

Sheila heard! Her heart fluttered. Would it, could it be possible? She drew closer to Liam.

"Is there a…a chance that…that we could escape?" Her words were scarcely audible.

"There's talk. Other than that I'm not sure," Liam replied. "Depends who lives through the storm." He hesitated before continuing. Could he trust this young girl, he asked himself.

"What do you mean?" she asked.

The pleading in her voice reassured him, "With fewer overseers and a French raiding party, anything is possible."

"If such an opportunity should occur, you would not forget to warn me?"

Again his heartstrings were touched, "I'll come for you myself, sweet Sheila."

****

The hours passed and with them the rains and the howling winds. It had been a night of terror and anguish. A horn sounded. Nobody moved.

Sheila opened her eyes. She must have slipped into a restless sleep during the early hours of the morning. There was an eerie silence about the place. The room seemed to have more light. The storm had passed! The winds had ceased! She looked around. Lifeless forms entangled in piles of debris; gaping holes in the roof; an entire wall had collapsed leaving jagged splintered beams exposed where once it had joined the roof. These sights and others horrified and frightened her. Was everyone dead? How could all this have happened without her knowledge?

And then she remembered. It had been a pleasant dream. She was at home once again with her family. A beautiful spring day. The birds filled the perfumed air with the sweetest music. Her beloved father at her side was explaining…The picture faded. She could remember no more.

Liam stirred, then got to his feet.

"You all right?" he enquired.

"Yes, I think so," came the whispered response.

"You stay here. I'll have a look around. See what's going on."

He moved carefully over the rubble and respectfully avoided any contact with those who were obviously dead.

Sheila watched him go and before he disappeared raised her voice, "Be careful."

Liam did not respond.

After what seemed hours, he returned. His face, particularly his eyes and the manner in which he conducted himself, could not conceal his troubled mind.

"Tell me, tell me, Liam," Sheila pleaded.

"I'm not sure you really want to know."

The horn sounded again in the distance. It was then that she thought of Netty. Where was she?

But Liam had made a decision. He would not obey the call to assemble. Instead he would avail himself of the moment to escape the plantation and make his way to the beach. He knew in his heart that the French would also avail of the chaos and confusion in the wake of the hurricane to raid the coasts of Barbados.

"Are you with me? It will be a risk but it's our only chance," he took her hand and raised her to her feet.

"Yes, yes! I'll do anything to leave this place," Sheila answered without hesitation.

Chapter 6

"Slavery is an atrocious debasement of human nature."
- Franklin

In 1657, Daniel Stearle was governor of Barbados. The Irish were central to the many revolts that had taken place over the years. All who were in the position of authority or who possessed property, be they merchants, planters, or government officials were fearful lest the island be taken over by such an uprising.

In November of '55 several Irish servants and slaves had banded together, and joined by a few blacks, ran away from their masters. The Council of Barbados was informed of this happening by Captain Richard Goodall and Mr. John Jones in the following words: "(They are) out in Rebellion in ye thicket and thereabouts." The Council ordered Lieutenant Colonel Higginbotham "to raise any of the companies of Colonel Henry Hawley's regiment, to follow ye said servants and runaway slaves, and if he shall meet with any of them, to cause them forthwith to be secured, and to send them before the Governor or some Justice of the Peace. But if any of the said servants and runaway Negroes make any opposition, and resist his forces, then to use his utmost endeavours to suppress or destroy them."

However these orders were not successfully carried out. As the records attest, the slaves, white and black, launched their own attacks. Using the machetes with which they cut the cane, they butchered many of their masters. They then took their arms and used them effectually on the militia who tried to hunt them down. They burned the sugar fields and the mills and warehouses. Those acts, of course, struck at the very heart of the economic structure of the island.

The uprising became so widespread and the number of rebel slaves – Irish and black – became so numerous, that the governor had to mobilize the entire militia. An act was passed in September of 1657 creating a law to "kill and destroy such runaways".

After several engagements in which many of the slaves fought to the bitter end preferring death to the inevitable tortures that awaited them were they caught, those who remained withdrew into the thickets. Among those captured there were six Irishmen who were locked in a cage in Bridgetown.

Hastily, a court was convened in which all those captured were condemned to death by fire.

In his book, *To Hell or Barbados*, Sean O'Callaghan best describes the ordeal:

On the appointed day a large crowd gathered to watch the sentence being carried out. Among them were some high-born ladies who were given ringside seats in a special area reserved for members of the Assembly and their guests. The prisoners, stark naked, were nailed to the ground in the form of a cross, with pegs of hardwood driven through their hands and feet. A burning torch was then applied to their feet and moved very slowly up their bodies. They were then beheaded and the heads were displayed on pikes in prominent positions in the marketplace. The owners were given £25 compensation for each man killed or executed.

Shortly after this event, the hurricane which devastated the Spencer plantation and wrecked the Big House gave the slaves who survived the chance to escape.

Rumours of French vessels plying the eastern waters quickly circulated among the slave population. It was in the hope of reaching the northeastern part of the island, as far away as possible from Bridgetown, that Liam and Sheila set out that morning.

It would be a journey fraught with dangers and hardships. But the pair was determined to succeed.

****

France and England had been at loggerheads for hundreds of years. It is no surprise then to find that the English settlers in the West Indies feared the consequences of a war with France. They knew that the Irish papists would, undoubtedly, try to find a means of escape to the French colonies. The Irish were known to have stowed away on vessels plying in the area. They had seized boats at night and set sail. Many had even disguised themselves as soldiers or sailors in order to board the military ships.

For the above reason, in 1652, some five years before Sheila had set foot on Barbadian soil, the governor, Daniel Searle, having the 'Bloody Papists' of Ireland in mind, issued the following order:

"Myself and the council having taken into consideration…the considerable number of Irish, freemen and servants, within this island, and the Dangerous consequences, in this Juncture of time, of Wars betwixt the Commonwealth of Englande and Spain both in Europe and here… that may ensue to this Place upon the appearance of an enemy, if the Irish and such others as are of the Romish Religion, should be permitted to have any sort of Arms or Ammunition within their Houses or Custody, or at anytime to wear or go Armed; have thought it necessary for the better security of this Place, and the continuance of Peace Thereof, to order, that all such as are of the Irish Nation...be forthwith Disarmed."

In case of an invasion, all the Irish were to be rounded up and kept in custody. Those in authority such as Church wardens in the respective parishes were required:

"to take account an exact list of all the Irish that live or bee in their Parishes, and such among them, as are of turbulent, seditious, troublesome, or dangerous spirits, that they returne the names of such to the Governor and Counsell upon Friday next, it being a business of great importency and concernment to the Peace and security of this Island."

Thereafter, even stricter and more severe measures were introduced. Yet the Irish persisted, many running away from their masters and mistresses. Laws were enacted whereby the runaways when caught were branded (first escape attempt), their ears cut off (second attempt), and finally executed, as a deterrent to other slaves.

Travelling by night, Liam and Sheila made their way to the coast on the west side of the island, to a cove near

St. Andrews. They were surprised to find a small group of other runaway slaves gathered in the same area.

Bruised and scarred from their journeying across cane-fields and rough terrain, they were now faced with a dilemma. The scraps of food they had managed to steal from their respective masters were in short supply. How long more could they exist? Yet they were determined to die rather than return to their lives of slavery.

"I'm afraid, Liam," said Sheila as she scanned the raging ocean for the sign of any craft. "Afeared we'll not be seeing Spanish or even English vessels in these waters." Then her gaze was directed to the crashing surf near the shoreline. "Even if a boat were to appear, how could it come close enough to rescue us?" She looked for the slightest sign of reassurance in Liam's face.

Liam realized that their only hope of survival was to join with a group which had already gathered in the restricted confines of the narrow strip of coastline. Somehow, the men-folk had to build a raft. Liam approached listening carefully to the spoken tongue. Were they Scots, Welsh, or English? For well he knew that there was a smattering of these folk on the island; many of whom were just as bitter against the plantation owners as the Irish slaves.

"Stay you here, lest there be trouble, Sheila. I'll give a signal signifying friend or foe."

Unfortunately, though the Scots and the Welsh were Celts by origin and blood, and therefore were more closely akin to the Irish than the race which conquered them, yet were they loath to join with their cousins, the Papists. The Celts, ever an independent race of people, did not always side with their own kind against a common enemy. Had they done so in times of war, the world would be a different place. For there were no braver warriors, or fighters more fierce in battle than the Celts.

Liam cautiously made his way among the rocks. To his relief and joy, he soon determined that the tongue he heard was that of his own countrymen.

He signaled Sheila, who quickly joined him and together they made their presence known to the group.

After another anxious day of waiting, hiding and trying to forage for food and with no sign of any vessel Spanish or French, the young men, of whom there were five, decided the only way they could escape the island was to build a raft.

Chapter 7

"Not only does the Christian religion, but Nature herself,
cry out against the state of slavery."
-Pope Leo X

Word of the runaway slaves reached into every miserable hut and makeshift shack. Reprisal would be swift and ruthless, of that the slaves were assured. Most, however, envied the escapees and prayed that they had made it to a better land.

In the days that followed, the estimated number of slaves who had escaped was duly recorded. Several bodies were later found but that fact did not change the number on the tally sheet. Thirty persons, men and women, had fled; several of whom, it was later discovered, had been picked up by a Spanish vessel that had been blown off course. Their eventual fate could only be surmised. The young men might be put to work on board the vessel and in time prove worthy ship-mates. Others, less fortunate, particularly those picked up by British ships would again be sold into slavery. The women, of course, found themselves in even more perilous plight; some forced to live a life worse than death, either on board ship or in the brothels on nearby islands. The few who considered themselves blessed might be bought by plantation owners of a more humane persuasion, ending up as housemaids in their manors.

One such escapee was Ann 'Goody' Glover, Sheila's friend and protector during the long sea voyage from Ireland to Barbados.

During the evening meal, in whispered tones, Ann had learned of the many revolts and escapes instigated by Irish slaves over the years. She never ceased to pray, and eagerly anticipated the day when she too would get the opportunity to cast aside the yolk of her humiliation. A miserable slave she would not remain for the rest of her life.

"God knows," she mumbled to herself, "if my poor Rory were alive, I'd be out o' this hell long ago." She convinced herself, remembering her dead husband, that things would have been very different had he been at her side. A strong vigorous young man he had been. True to his Catholic beliefs, he never wavered and outwardly professed his faith. It was for his strong faith, and his unquestionable adherence to Catholicism and not the minor transgression of which he was accused, that the overseer had him beaten to death.

Since that time, Ann had kept to herself as much as she could and tried to avoid any confrontation with those in authority. Although she too was a strong papist, she considered her duty was to live for her only child and bide her time. But she would be alert. When the very first opportunity came her way to make good her promise to herself, she would avail of it. She would escape! Yes, she would take the chance, escape or die trying.

****

After the restoration of the monarchy in England, King Charles the Second took over more direct control of the government of the English colonies. The Governor was appointed directly by the King; the Council appointed by the Governor from members of the landed class. These members advised the Governor, made the laws and voted the taxes. The Governor of Barbados became the Governor-General of the Leeward Islands and was responsible for their defense. In return for this protection and the confirmation of their titles to the land, the Colonial Assemblies consented to a 4.5% duty on their exports to cover the cost of royal government.

In 1665 France joined the Dutch against the English over control of the African slave trade. War broke out and many of the Leeward islands were invaded. Barbados, however, did not experience this intrusion. Mayor John Scott leaves the following description of the island:

> Barbados is the Crown and Front of all the Caribbean islands towards the rising sun, being the most east of any and lies more conveniently of the rest for a seat of war, being most healthful, fruitful and stored with all things necessary for life. It is the great mart of trade, inhabited by many merchants and planters and in time of war is free from the danger of any enemy.

Indeed, Barbados in the 17th century was the Sugar Revolution or the large-scale production of cane sugar on large farms or 'plantations' owned and managed by Englishmen who brought thousands of Africans as well as Irishmen, women and children to the island as slaves. Few people today realize that from the early 1600s and for most of the 17th century, far more Irish were sold as slaves than Africans in the West Indies.[12]

---

12   Little known facts – In the mid 1600's "52,000 Irish, mostly women, boys and girls were sold to Barbados and Virginia. Another 30,000 men and women were taken prisoners and sold as slaves, while in 1688 Cromwell's Council of State ordered that 1,000 Irish girls and 1,000 Irish boys be rounded up and taken to Jamaica to be sold as slaves to English planters. As horrendous as

This was the period when Barbados became the most valuable piece of real estate in the entire world. It even became known as the place where Sugar was 'King.'

Over the years, as Barbados was never invaded, the island prospered, and with stability it was the chief 'jewel in the King of England's Crown,' gaining for itself the title of Little England.

However, despite the island's relative stability, the island did have its own set of problems. The Spanish and French pirates sailed menacingly close to its shores and turbulent weather at times decimated the crops, precipitating African and Irish slave revolts. It was during the chaos that followed attempted raids or violent hurricanes that the slaves availed of the opportunities to move about which in turn allowed them to pass on vital information to other 'rebels.' This tension generated fear and anxiety among the slave owners and fueled the hatred of the Irish who were blamed as the instigators. No mercy was shown when these 'wild savages' were caught.

****

Ten long years had passed in the pitiful life of Ann 'Goody' Glover before her chance came to make good her promise to herself. But fate finally gave her the opportunity for which she had so ardently prayed and waited.

"The night was black as a jackdaw's wing," were the words Ann used when she told of her escape.

"Eileen was but a young girl at the time. I had heard that a Dutch ship was anchored in the bay. Somehow, I knew I had to get myself and my child on board that vessel."

---

these numbers sound, it only reflects a small part of the evil program, as most of the slaving, actually was not recorded." (Robert E. West, PEC Ill. State Director) <u>England's Irish Slaves</u>.

Ann continued her story: "When I was sure all around me were sleeping soundly, I gathered up what few things I had and together with my daughter, I ran as fast as I could towards the harbour. Only one lantern was alight on the ship. I was lucky; the gangplank was down. Very quietly and quickly we made our way along the wharf and up onto the ship."

'Goody,' as she was known to her friends, of whom she had few being a papist and Irish, paused a moment as she recollected the moment. Even after all the years since that fateful night, she still felt the tension, the fear, the anxiety… "Only God knows how I climbed that gang-plank, how I reached the safety of a stack of barrels. Barrels of raw sugar, they were. But a welcome protection for me and my girl in the darkness."

Again she hesitated. "We were well out to sea the next day before we were discovered."

"Ye were fortunate. I'm surprised the captain didn't have ye all thrown overboard. Ye wouldn't ha' been the first, ye know," her friend interjected.

"Aye, indeed I know that. But God was with us. Maybe me dead Rory was lookin' after us." She crossed herself.

"It was the Captain's boy who found us. At the top of his voice, he yelled: 'Stowaways, Captain! Captain Bogers, we've got two slaves on board, females they are, Sir.'"

Ann continued, "'Bring 'em here, Boy,' the Captain ordered. The Captain did not leave his post at the helm or even turn his head.

"We slowly made our way to the bow of the ship. The Captain took his pipe from his mouth, blew a whiff and turned his head slightly. Barely glancing at us, he said, 'Hah, so these skin-flints ha' come aboard to eat their way to Boston!'

"'No, Sir,' I answered.

"'No! 'Tis dumpin' ye overboard, I've a mind to do,' was his response.

"'Now that might be a mistake, Sir.' I spoke with determination.

"The Captain turned his full gaze on us. 'How so?' he asked.

"'Ye see, Sir, I'm a great cook, been cookin' in the Big House for nigh on ten years. Aye, seen many a fine party in me time.' I could see me words were havin' an effect.

"'That so.' The Captain paused. 'I'll give you an' the girl a few days to prove yer worth. Get below an' start cookin' an' it better be good.'

"I was about to say, 'A workman can only do what his tools will allow,' but thought the better of it. I caught Eileen be the hand and turned me back on Captain Bogers.

"That evenin' the Captain an' crew had the first decent meal in over two months. André, the dethroned master of the galley, wasn't happy but when I managed to give him an extra portion and told him he would have his old job back as soon as the ship reached Boston, he was somewhat comforted. And again I thanked God for his mercy to me and me girl. We would live to see a better day."

Boston, a sprawling settlement, was a welcome sight when Captain Bogers docked in its murky waters on the morning of June 14th, 1668.

Part II

Montserrat

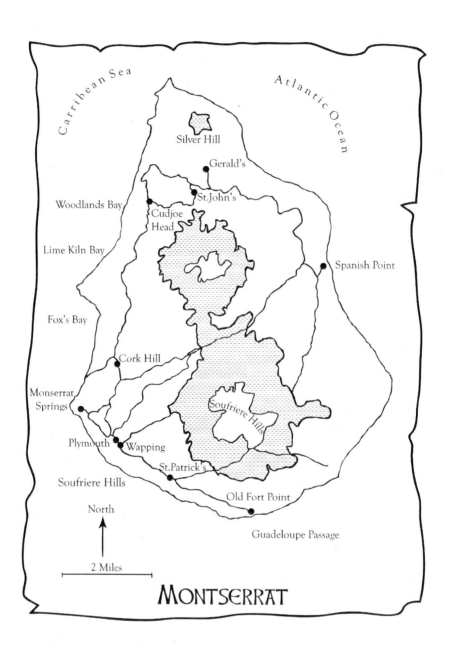

Carribean Sea

Atlantic Ocean

Silver Hill

Gerald's

St.John's

Woodlands Bay

Cudjoe Head

Lime Kiln Bay

Spanish Point

Fox's Bay

Cork Hill

Monserrat Springs

Soufriere Hills

Plymouth   Wapping

St.Patrick's

Soufriere Hills

Old Fort Point

North

Guadeloupe Passage

2 Miles

MONTSERRAT

Chapter 8

"Drunkenness is nothing else but a voluntary madness."

- *Seneca*

Upon a sliver of a beach with the waters lapping in ceaseless abandon, they found her. Whether or not there was life in her, at first, they were not sure.

A black slave, muscular and strong, a man named Ben, lifted her limp body from the rocks and carried her to the Big House – the home away from home of the Governor, Roger Osborne. Osborne had been appointed to be the administrator of the island of Montserrat as well as the other Leeward isles in 1650.

In 1651, the English Parliament passed the first of the Navigation Acts, attempting to end the trade with the Dutch in the West Indies. But Osborne paid no heed to this Act and consequently trade with the Dutch continued. He, of course, benefitted handsomely from these transactions with the Dutch, stocking special warehouses with European goods which he later sold for huge profits. But, more anon. For Osborne's story is long. A tale of deeds dark and dastardly.

****

The party was set to begin in the late afternoon. Those invited had arrived early to avoid the heat of the midday sun. Some had even come the evening before. The carriages had drawn up at the great front entrance. A liveried footman opened the carriage doors to allow the ladies and fine gentlemen to alight. And as the uniformed slaves appeared to carry in the baggage, the haughty guests quickly made their way into the entrance hall ceaselessly chatting and with much pretense greeting those already assembled there.

A light repast was served around noon and, soon after, all repaired to their respective rooms for the usual siesta, a repose of approximately two hours.

"You know, my dear," Charles Prendergast addressed his wife, Liza, when they were alone in their bed-chamber, "I've made this journey with much reservation and some trepidation."

"Why so?" Liza sat looking out a window that offered an expansive view of the bay and the 'new Fort' at Kinsale. A few ships anchored in the calm waters seemed as listless as the rest of the world around them. Nothing moved. The sun poised in the mid-day sky stared steadfastly and relentlessly upon the baked clay-pavement, cracked and dusty. The heavy humid tropical air held a tight firm grip on the world of nature. Liza sighed as she fanned herself. She felt the perspiration ooze from every pore of her body. Taking a dainty kerchief from a pocket in her gown, she mopped the drops of moisture from her brow before she turned to face her husband.

"I dislike introducing Beth to…" he was about to list the names of the young bucks whom he disliked.

"Tut, tut," his wife interrupted. "You have said that before, my dear. But how on earth will the girl ever meet an eligible suitor in this backwoods, if we don't attend some of these receptions?"

"She should return to England."

"She is our responsibility, not Julia's. My sister was kind enough to take her while she attended the academy but now…" Liza got up and approached the bed where her husband had already stretched his muscular body. A man in his late forties, he was still in his prime with energy and a verve for the better things in life – the attention of young women being one of them.

Liza, on the other hand, had aged in the ten years she had spent on the island. Although in her early forties, her dark brown hair had streaks of grey, and conceal it as she might try, it was obvious to all. Crows feet had appeared in the corners of her pretty blue eyes and her once creamy soft skin had taken on a jaundiced cast. What with the running of a large household of slaves and servants, the responsibility of raising four unruly children (two boys and two girls), and having no compatible female companionship, she, unlike her husband, resented the restrains and isolation that living on the island had created for her.

Accustomed to a sophisticated lifestyle in high society in her native England, the existence Liza experienced in the 'backwood' of tropical Montserrat had taken its toll. When she complained to her husband that the piano was out of tune, that her favorite books were falling apart from mildew and insects, his only reply was: "My dear, what do you expect? This is not England."

Though Charles seemed indifferent to his wife's complaints, the fact remained that there really was little he could do, short of shipping his whole family back to the motherland. Consequently, he was loath to see his oldest daughter, Beth, who had recently returned from a four-year finishing school in England, trapped in the same conditions.

Liza lay beside her husband. As usual she could not sleep. It was too hot. So she allowed her thoughts to wander as she listened to the rhythmic snores on the other side of the bed. She, like her husband Charles, was not in favour of participating in the Osborne societal functions. But as part of the upper class on the island, it was expected of them and of course on this particular occasion there was the ulterior motive of their oldest daughter's future.

The rumours were rife regarding the conduct of the Governor who had been confirmed in 1663 by the First Legislative Assembly elected under the new form of government. King Charles the Second, it must be remembered, took a more direct interest in and control of the English colonies, thus Osborne was not just any Governor of Barbados, but Governor-General of the Leewards as well and responsible for their defense. So he took it upon himself to visit these 'far-flung outposts' as he called them, on occasion.

Liza had heard of the Samuel Waad case. Waad, a wealthy English planter, owned three large plantations on the island of Montserrat, a sugar works, and 50 slaves. He had married Elizabeth Osborne Brisket, the widow of Governor Anthony Brisket and thereby came into the control of Brisket's lands as well as his own. Only two years later, Elizabeth died. Governor Osborne, who was her brother, now saw his chance to take control of all these lands. He provoked an argument with Waad who, in turn, called him an 'Irish barbarian' and an 'Irish murderer.'

Osborne had Waad immediately arrested and thrown in prison. Within a few days he had him shot to death. Osborne then confiscated all Waad's property, including his harvested crops of sugar and tobacco, but in the name of Anthony Brisket II, who was his nephew and ward. However, it was Osborne, the Governor, who held the lands.

As Liza pondered this, other stories came to mind. "A bully, a drunkard and a scoundrel," were the words used by Morris West, a neighbour of theirs in the northwest, when he was describing Roger Osborne. And he continued, "Yet, he lives in comfort, nay, luxury in Barbados most of the year where he holds the highest office in the British colonies. His household alone requires the services of several bakers, many grooms and seamstresses. I'm told, he even boasts a midwife! No doubt he has need of her, if his nightly adventures are to be believed. And, of course, he has a butler, six or seven white pages to run his errands and the pick of the female slaves lately arriving from Ireland."

Liza remembered hearing that even the slaves, who were aware of him only by name, were fearful of him. His lust and cruelty and his drunken brawls were constant subjects of their conversation. Among the plantation owners, like herself and her husband, his avarice and ceaseless quest for power were topics frequently discussed – *sotto voce.*

****

The Big House, as it was called, was well-built. Fashioned after the English style, it had many glass windows and doors, mullioned for the most part. Inside, the furnishings and décor were opulent. Silverware, crystal candelabra and elegant furniture all chosen with taste and at considerable expense offered a life-style of ease and comfort for the master, his mistress and their children.

It was to this household that the semi-conscious young woman, for as yet there was no knowledge of her name, was delivered. Bridget, the housekeeper, immediately took charge. Bridget, although an Irish woman, had control of the many slaves, black and white, that were employed in the Manor. She was considered superior to the lowly slaves, although she worked without pay, for she was an indentured servant. She had arrived on the island several years prior to the vast majority of the Irish slaves who were presently being transported there. When she had arrived, she could not count on being treated differently from the other slaves, but she had hope on her side. One day, when her tenure expired, usually ten to fifteen years, she could receive her freedom.

As the years passed, the island of Montserrat, being quite removed from Barbados, grew increasingly self-reliant. The local plantation owners became wealthy as the sugar market expanded. Many of these planters were English, and a few of them owned negro slaves. The small coastal trading centers developed around Brisket's Bay, Plymouth and Kinsale. But the indentured servants of Irish descent who had received their just deserts – freedom after years of service without pay – were also making progress and had improved their living standards. Many had acquired small holdings, built more suitable dwelling places and married. Bridget was one such person.

When Governor Osborne was not in residence, his estate in Montserrat was under the control of an overseer, a Mr. Henry Ashbury. Now Mr. Ashbury did not hold his position lightly. A man of discipline, honest and forthright, he was also a shrewd calculating fellow. Observing how skillfully and smoothly Bridget managed the household, he was duly impressed. Rarely did she have any grave difficulties with the slaves, mostly female, or the other indentured servants. A union with such a woman would only strengthen his position. He regarded her physical appearance with a critical eye. A plain face, no doubt, but not completely unattractive. She had alert grey-blue eyes, a straight nose, and yes, one could say shapely lips. Furthermore, since she had her own quarters within the Manor, the move from his miserable abode among the slaves, to those superior quarters would be a welcome change. Yes, a man could do much worse, he conjectured. He marked well her temperament and concluded that she was a woman of temperate ways. All in all, he was satisfied that the correct decision was his.

****

Bridget knew at once she was dealing with a young woman of refined and gentle upbringing. Undoubtedly she was Irish. Captured like so many others, she was probably destined for the slave markets of Barbados or Jamaica when the ship that was transporting her was wrecked.

Bridget was moved. So young! So beautiful! But she must not show her true feelings. She ordered that the girl be placed on the floor out of the way of the slaves going about their household duties.

"Aye, that will do. I'll take a look at her. Probably not worth savin' anyway."

As soon as Ben had departed, Bridget undid the wet clothing and wrapped the chilled body in a sheet. She rubbed her hands and feet and tried to drip a few drops of water into her mouth.

After some moments, Bridget's efforts were rewarded, when a low moan escaped the prone figure. Then slowly she opened her eyes.

"Well, well," Bridget spoke gently and in the Irish tongue, "Ye have come back to the land of the living, may God be praised."

Sheila, reassured by the sounds of her native language, tried to answer, but no sound came.

"Rest now. You're safe. We'll talk anon," Bridget answered her silent plea.

When she had recovered, Bridget called two female slaves and had them carry the young woman to a couch in one of the parlors. For several days, she took care of her personally, until she was sufficiently restored to health and able to tell her own story.

Bridget was drawn to the young woman. Her maternal instinct aroused, she wished to protect her.

Together, they agreed to keep her life on the island of Barbados a secret. No one should ever know that she had been a slave. Educated and refined, she had been, as Bridget had concluded, a child of privilege. Unfortunately, the traumatic experiences of her recent past obliterated all memory of her previous life. This was the story that would be noised abroad.

When word reached Montserrat of the Governor's impending visit, Bridget decided it was time to part with Sheila. Had Mr. Osborne ever laid eyes on the lovely Sheila, she would be forever enslaved, a plaything in his own household. Enquiries were made.

The Callaghan household in the north was in dire need of a governess. What with six children whose education was closely supervised, a large domestic staff consisting of cooks, laundry slaves, cleaning maids, and the male slaves who maintained the kitchen gardens and the cooking fires, Mistress Callaghan had little leisure time to devote to entertainment. Yet this necessity was expected of her. Isolated in a backward island, those of the upper class had few recreational alternatives. Even books were scarce commodities, and those fortunate to possess a few could hardly keep them protected and intact. Mildew and curious tropical insects quickly wrought havoc on the binding and the discoloured yellowish paper. As a consequence pages fell out, and those which remained bore holes of varying sizes. Conversation, genial or otherwise, was the recognized release from the humdrum lives most endured in what the rest of the world considered a tropical paradise.

So it was that amid the hustle and bustle in preparation for the Governor's visit, a carriage arrived to transport Sheila to the Callaghan estate some sixty miles to the north of Plymouth.

Chapter 9

*"Those sold to the heretics in America are treated by
them more cruelly than the slaves under the Turks; nor is
any attention paid to youth or the decrepitude of old age,
to sex or rank, to sacerdotal orders to religious life."*

> -   *Cardinal Giovanni Rinuccini,*
> Papal Nuncio to the
> Confederation of Kilkenny (1645-
> 1648*)*

The guests had assembled in a large reception room.
Many were happy to renew old acquaintances, while a few
were newcomers. Among the latter was Beth Prendergast,
the blush of youth and innocence on her fair cheeks. Beth
had just turned seventeen, which was considered a suitable
age for any prospective bachelor to cast his eyes in her
direction.

Charles Prendergast looked around; most of those present
were Catholic and Irish. Determination was written on their
faces. They had risen from servitude and squalor in the
last ten years to become landowners and persons of status.
These men and women, however, did have an advantage
over the vast majority of their countrymen. They had been
indentured servants. In other words they had come to the
islands of their own volition and signed up to work for a
fixed number of years. Having fulfilled their obligation,
they had obtained their freedom and gone forth to build
their own lives.

Charles Prendergast was proud of his achievements. And he knew the rest of his friends who gathered together that night were also proud of their accomplishments.

His attention was drawn to several young men who had gravitated to one corner. A hearty laugh from a rather boisterous fellow carried over the chatter of the ladies. Charles approached the group; his wife being engaged in deep conversation with an old friend, Alice Parker.

"Allow me to introduce myself, gentlemen. Charles Prendergast from the St. John's area," he offered his hand to the youth beside him. As he did, he noticed one member of the group moved away.

"Henry Mason," the young man answered and shook his hand. "And this is my good friend, Daniel Stokes. For Mr. John Scott, I cannot vouch, Sir, having made his acquaintance not five minutes hence." He addressed the flamboyant gentleman facing him.

At that juncture, the young man, John Scott, again laughed aloud and then answered, "These gentlemen, I determine, have formed no great opinion of me. And so quickly! Whereas, I have not yet determined the depths of their characters. It takes time to know the true temper of a man, think you not, Sir?"

"With that I would concur, Mr. Scott. But tell me, gentlemen, you were a group of four as I approached. Wherefore did your friend depart?"

"Oh! You're referring no doubt to Hall, Edmund Hall. A rare bird if ever there was one. Taciturn, brooding and cautious. But I'll say one thing for him, he's loaded."

"Oh! Strange, I've not heard of him before. Not that any of you young men are known to me. But you know the saying, 'money talks.' And besides, I'm from the backwoods and news travels slowly to our parts."

"It's not surprising, Sir, that you have not heard of Hall. He has but lately arrived in these parts. It is said that he owns a large estate in the south of England. Surrey, I think. At present, he is traveling with the Governor."

"I see. Well I'm happy to have made your acquaintance, gentlemen." Charles looked around. "I see my wife is in need of my attention. I presume none of you are as yet bound in the holy state of matrimony?"

The young men laughed. Then Mr. Scott replied, "Heaven forbid. I, for one, need my freedom a little longer. Time enough to take on the cares and troubles of the domestic life."

"Aye, aye," the friends added.

"Then I bid you a good evening, gentlemen. Perhaps we'll meet again ere the night is o'er." With these words Charles withdrew.

But before he joined his wife, he allowed his eyes to wander around the room again, this time in search of the elusive Mr. Hall.

He stood alone, apart from the throng. As if sizing up the assembly, his dark eyes moved slowly from one group to another. The ladies were of particular interest. A slight smirk teased his countenance a fleeting moment and then he decided, or it appeared so, that he had had enough. He turned to leave the room. At that juncture, Charles Prendergast approached him.

"I've not had the honour of being introduced to you, Sir."

"By now, you no doubt know my name. Yours...."

"Charles Prendergast." Somewhat piqued by the reply, Charles nevertheless maintained his dignity.

"Now that we've been introduced you'll allow me." With that Mr. Hall left the room.

"Snob, insolent snob," the words were audible but Charles didn't care.

Word of Mr. Hall's behaviour soon circulated. And before the evening was spent, there were many who despised him.

"Too good for the likes of us. That's what he thinks. Well, we have had enough of his kind," said Mistress Prendergast when her husband informed her of Mr. Hall's conduct. She immediately informed her friend, Alice Parker, who in turn was only too happy to spread the word.

Meanwhile, the despised Mr. Hall had repaired to an adjacent sitting room, an area obviously set apart for the men. It was furnished with an ample liquor supply, as well as cigars, card and backgammon tables. Hall poured himself a drink and sat down.

"What a life!" he allowed his thoughts a voice. He scanned the perimeters of the room. A bookcase caught his attention. He laid his glass aside and rising went to explore. A man's taste in reading material spoke more of his character than the many words he uttered. Opening the glass door, he glimpsed the first title: *History of England in the Reign of Henry VIII*. Plato's *Republic* stood boldly beside it. He took the tome from the shelf but, as soon as he opened it up, several pages fell to the floor. As he tried to pick them up, the paper disintegrated. They were riddled with holes of varying sizes.

"A world rotten and decaying before our very eyes!" he mumbled.

He was interrupted from making further comment by a servant bearing a lighted taper. Darkness was quickly descending; soon the room would be completely enveloped in darkness. Another reminder that he was in the tropics.

He returned the book to its place, closed the chest and as the servant departed, returned to his seat. He would relax for a while. The night would be long, and with no penchant for cards or backgammon, and the conversation boring to say the least, he was not at all convinced he could stomach it. Another glass of Rum might make the intolerable tolerable.

Just as Mr. Hall was about to doze, the door was thrown open and two young women ran into the room, flung themselves onto a sofa and burst into peels of laughter. They did not see Mr. Hall at the other end of the room. When they gained control of themselves, they began to talk.

"Did you ever in your life see such a foolish fellow?" a girl with dark ringlets dancing as she spoke asked.

Her companion, fair of face and hair, replied, "Nor do I ever again want to meet the likes."

They giggled again.

Mr. Hall had had enough. "Lest you say something you ladies might later regret, I must alert you to my presence. Ladies, allow me to introduce myself."

Beth Prendergast and Charlotte Everston, for they were the two young women Mr. Hall now faced, were dumbstruck. They sat bolt upright with their mouths open.

"Ladies," Mr. Hall continued, "my name is Edmund Hall," he bowed slightly.

Beth was the first to find her tongue. "Mr. Hall, I'm pleased to make your acquaintance. This is my friend

Charlotte Everston, and I'm Beth Prendergast. We had no idea you were here and did not mean to disturb you."

Hall gazed into the upturned innocent blue eyes and was strangely affected. Making an effort to overcome what seemed a natural attraction, Edmund stepped backward. Unfortunately, there was a footstool which he had not noticed right behind him.

The result caused him considerable embarrassment. The girls looked shocked but had to place their hands over their mouths to stop themselves from laughing. However, to his credit, Mr. Hall got to his feet, brushed himself off and making light of the situation promptly seated himself close by.

"It gives me satisfaction to have been the cause of your amusement, ladies." Smiling, he continued, "If it pleases you further, I would like to know more about you." He was looking straight into Beth's eyes, "Your homes, your families, your lives here on this backward island. Ladies such as you must find the time tedious, long, boring, and besides there are so few prospects for you. By that I mean eligible young men. As women, your future seems to me bleak." He paused a moment as if pondering the awful reality, then added, "Is it not so?"

"Not at all. Not so bleak as you might think, Mr. Hall. We find pleasure in the company of each other, our female friends, you know. Men are not the only beacons of light in our lives," Beth answered with a rather haughty air. But there was a soft, rather expressive ray from her eyes. It said much.

Hall was not indifferent. Happy, simple in demeanor, innocent as a newborn, he was not willing to be parted from her so soon. For having delivered her opinion, Beth rose to leave. It would not be considered prudent, or ladylike, after all, to be seen conversing in a room apart from the other guests with a complete stranger.

Hall stood aside to allow the girls to pass. They quickly returned to the main assembly hall just in time to be presented to the Governor and his wife.

As Beth stepped forward and curtsied, the Governor's eyes grew wide with interest. Not that Beth was particularly beautiful, but she was young and had a shapely body. Her eyes were her most striking features. And besides, the Governor had grown tired of matronly faces and the bodies, flabby and wrinkled. This young thing was attractive.

"You must pay us a visit soon in Plymouth, my dear. My wife and I would be most pleased to see you and show you the sights of our prospering town."

"Thank you, Sir, for your invitation," Beth would say no more. Having heard of Roger Osborne's many dalliances, not to mention his fondness for 'the bottle,' the young girl was on her guard. But as the Governor persisted, she answered, "Such an invitation, Sir, deserves my father's consent." With that she quickly withdrew giving her place to the next in line.

After what was considered a lavish meal, the ladies withdrew to a parlor apart from their men-folk. A few card tables were available, but the younger members were the only ladies interested. The older, more sophisticated women seated themselves in groups of preference and resumed the topics of conversation which had been interrupted earlier by the seating arrangements in the dining room.

Someone, eventually, tried to perform on the pianoforte, but it was so badly out of tune that the artist was forced to abandon it, and that with a loud thud of the cover lest the ugly discoloured keys be observed.

Mr. Hall was not seen for the remainder of the evening. Where he had hidden himself was a mystery. Although an hour of dancing took place in the ballroom accompanied by a few musicians from the Governor's mansion in Plymouth, Mr. Hall did not put in an appearance. Beth was rather disappointed, although she would not admit it to herself.

But the following morning bright and early, she again chanced to meet him at breakfast.

"Good morning, Miss Prendergast," he studied her a moment, "You look radiant. I trust you slept very well."

"Thank you, Mr. Hall. Yes, I did have a good night's sleep and that despite the buzzing of the mosquitoes."

They both laughed. Heads turned and older folk exchanged glances.

"You know, it's impossible to talk here." He bent toward her, and said in a more whispered tone, "Meet me in the garden within the hour, I would have a word with you in private." Then remembering his position and hers, he added, "Please, I need to know." Then he turned on his heels and walked out of the room.

Beth blushed as she took her place at the breakfast table. For a moment she fumbled with her fruit plate.

Then an older woman's voice reached her ears, "Perhaps she knows Mr. Hall from her school days in England. You know, young girls these days don't spend all their leisure hours reading and riding."

The jab was severe.

Beth hung her head a moment, but then decided she would fight back, "That remark was unnecessary and not worthy of whomever made it. I will have you know that Mr.

Hall is as much a stranger to me as he is to everyone else here this morning." With that she too left the room intent on confronting Mr. Hall and putting him in his place for the embarrassment he had caused her.

Chapter 10

"No man is free who is not master of himself."

- Epictetus

It was dark when Sheila McCarthy arrived at the Callaghan estate. The family had already retired for the night. Only the housekeeper, Mrs. Cole, was available to welcome her and show her directly to her room.

Her room, her own room! Although small in comparison with the room she shared with her sister in the McCarthy castle, it was a far cry from the hard dirt floor she had endured for the past six years in Barbados.

Exhausted, she laid her small cloth bag which carried her night attire and nothing else on the chair. No one had given any thought to her well-being. Not even Mrs. Cole, who seemed a kindly woman, asked her if she were hungry or in need of anything.

As soon as Mrs. Cole bade her good-night and closed the door, Sheila went on her knees and thanked God for her deliverance from slavery and the chance to better herself.

She had a bed! A real bed and it was fitted with a mosquito net! Such luxury. At last she would be able to get a good night's sleep.

The following morning, Mrs. Cole had to awaken her.

"Mistress Callaghan will see you within the hour in the morning room." The good woman laid a tray on the small table close by the bed. It contained a bowl of fruit, a cup of tea and a slice of bread.

"Thank you so much," Sheila was surprised at the gesture.

"When you are dressed, please come downstairs and I will take you to the Mistress."

"All right, I won't be long," replied Sheila.

She dressed quickly in her grey plain cotton frock, coiled her braided flaxen hair neatly around her head, and having made up her bed, set things to right in the room and made her way to the entrance hall.

As she did so, her thoughts turned to her native land and the life she had lost. She was grateful for one thing however, her early education. Although she was only twelve when she was savagely snatched away from her home, she had acquired many skills that would now enable her to surmount most difficulties. She could read and now speak the English language although it irked her to do so.

She held herself with dignity and elegance and went to meet the lady of the house.

"Good morning, Miss Sheila. It seems you have not yet remembered your last name. At least, that's what I'm given to believe," a slight raising of the eyebrows displayed doubt.

"Good morning, Mam," Sheila ignored the gesture. "Yes, your information is correct," she answered politely but with assurance. She would never again be treated as a slave.

"Well, be that as it may, I'm in sore need of a governess, having six children to educate. Two are already abroad or you would have been charged with eight. Now, since I have no references as to your background or the quality of your education, I will hire you only on a temporary basis." Mistress Callaghan hardly stopped for breath. Meantime, Sheila stood before her like a soldier awaiting orders.

"If I find after a suitable period of time, say six months, that you have discharged your duties to my satisfaction, and that my children have advanced in their studies, then we will come to, shall we say, more permanent arrangements. For now, and the next six months, you will receive a salary of ten shillings a month as well as food and board. Is that agreeable?"

Mistress Callaghan, having delivered her words in a forthright manner, now relaxed and lay back against her chair. She was still cold and aloof and did not allow her gaze to stray from Sheila's.

But the young woman did not cower. She stood her ground, and holding her head high, answered her new mistress respectfully, but mindful of whom she really was, she did not show condescension or subservience.

"Madam, you will not be disappointed with my efforts. I will begin immediately. If you will but introduce me to your children."

"All in good time. First I would have you inspect the study-hall and see if you have what you require to execute your work in an orderly and proficient manner."

Madam Callaghan maintained her authoritative posture, demonstrating clearly who it was that would really be in charge of that study-hall.

"Of course, Mam." Sheila answered somewhat stung by the rebuke. Obviously a good teacher would need to check her materials and environment before her students were presented to her.

Madam Callaghan rang for the housekeeper, Mrs. Cole. When that good woman made her appearance, she ordered her to accompany Miss Sheila to the study-hall.

"Before you depart, I want you to report to me directly what it is the children require. You will give me an accounting each week of the progress of each child," with these words Madam Callaghan dismissed her.

Undaunted, Sheila repaired to the study-hall to inspect the books and other materials on hand. Later that day, she presented Madam Callaghan with a list which included basics such as quills and graphite sticks. Of course these things would take time to acquire; in the meantime she was to make do with what she had.

The next day the children assembled in the classroom and Sheila was introduced to them. They ranged in ages from fourteen to two years old. Anna was the oldest child still at home: her two brothers, Liam and Sean, were in a boarding school in England. Next came Moire who was twelve. Three boys followed: Patrick, Rory, and Kevin, ages ten, nine, and eight. Little Eithne was five and baby Erin two years old. In all Sheila would be responsible for six of them.

Her first impressions caused her some misgivings. The girls she concluded would be easily controlled, but the boys...particularly Patrick and Rory! Constantly seeking attention, these two were full of mischief, and as time would tell, paid little or no attention to their lessons.

Sheila knew it was incumbent upon her to find a solution to this dilemma else she would be without a position and cast out without mercy.

One day, as she watched the two at play, she noticed that Patrick liked to pretend that he was a sea captain while Rory continually thought of himself as a soldier.

In a flash, she knew what she had to do. That same evening, she approached the lady of the house. Knocking on the door of Madam Callaghan's private sitting room, she heard the lady's voice, "Come in."

Opening the door, Sheila entered, "Begging your pardon, Mam, I have a request to make of you. You are aware that the boys Patrick and Rory are not inclined to pay too much attention to their lessons."

"That's your duty. Find a way to overcome that trivia; no doubt they are not the first children to have an aversion to learning certain subjects."

"You are correct, Mam..."

Mistress Callaghan interrupted, "They are young. In time, they will mature."

"Of course, Mam. But I've an idea which may encourage them to read, which as you know they seem to have an aversion to doing."

"Yes, yes," Mistress Callaghan was growing impatient. "What is it you require?"

Up to this time, Sheila had not asked for anything for the schoolroom except the bare essentials. And by and large, the mistress was pleased with her efforts.

However Sheila's present request caught the lady of the house by surprise.

"What an unusual approach!" she exclaimed.

As an incentive for the young boys, Sheila had suggested that books appertaining to life in the navy and naval vessels be obtained for Patrick and for his brother, literature capturing the flavour of army life and heroic acts. Furthermore, having perceived that both children were clever with their hands, Sheila intimated that using them in a constructive manner – building model ships or constructing a fort from wood, provided they learn to spell and learn the technical words appertaining to parts of ships, weapons, etc., might prove an additional stimulant, or motivator.

Reluctantly, Madam Callaghan agreed to the 'experiment' as she called it, but only for a limited period. The time-honoured method of teaching children either by rote or the more persuasive cane were her idea of tutoring the young.

Several weeks later, Madam decided to pay an unannounced visit to the schoolroom. Expecting to hear the usual din and commotion, she hesitated before entering the room.

All was quiet. Too quiet! Were the children sleeping? she asked herself. Well, if that were the case... She was paying a governess to supervise sleeping children... She flung the door wide.

Her mouth dropped open, her eyes opened wide. Not a word could she utter...

Every child was seriously concentrated on his or her task. Even little Eithne seated on the governess' lap was reading her homemade book, a story composed by Miss Sheila about a black cat.

"Ah, ahem," Madam Callaghan made known her presence.

As soon as five year-old Eithne saw her mother, her face lit up. "Mama, Mama, I can read. Then jumping to her feet, she ran to her mother carrying her treasured book. "Look Mama, my book! Miss Sheila made it special for me! An' I can read it all myself."

"Excellent, you have done a fine job. I've been listening to you, darling," Madam Callaghan's countenance was completely transformed.

By now the other children had raised their heads in anticipation of words of praise for their efforts also. All except Patrick and Rory who were completely absorbed in their handiwork.

At length, the Mistress of the house had to inquire what it was they were so taken with. Then the boys eagerly explained what to their mother was a complete mystery.

"I have to say, Miss Sheila, you are achieving far beyond my expectation. I must give credit where credit is due." Then she addressed the children, "Since you have been working so hard and have been following Miss Sheila's orders, I think it only right to award you all with a special treat."

The children with one voice cried, "Yah, yah, a treat!"

"How would you like to join me in half an hour for drinks and biscuits?"

"Hurrah!" was their unanimous reply.

****

Sheila's worth had risen a hundred percent in the eyes of Mistress Callaghan. Henceforth, she treated her with respect and was more open to her suggestions, even seeking her advice on occasion. And thus life had become much easier for Sheila. As time passed, although she sorely missed her family and her country, yet she considered herself fortunate, very fortunate indeed, to have escaped the bondage of slavery in Barbados.

Chapter 11

"He alone has lost the art to live who cannot win new friends."

- S. Walter Mitchell

The friendship between the lady of the house, Mistress Callaghan, and Sheila grew steadily. They spent many pleasant hours in lively conversation when the children had finished their schoolwork and Sheila had some leisure time. More and more, since Mr. Callaghan was frequently away on business, 'Mistress C,' as Sheila called her, would summon the young governess to her private sitting room to enjoy a cup of tea and some sweet cake. During those moments, the future of her children was discussed, some major decisions made, and plans set in motion for important activities. One such activity was the coming-of-age ball in honour of Anna.

Anna had grown into a fine young woman – not what one would call pretty but certainly attractive. At sixteen, she had good carriage; she was tall and slender. Her brown hair fell in gentle waves to her shoulders, but as she grew older, she liked to wear it caught up behind with a clasp. She had blue eyes, a shapely nose and firm lips. A mature young lady for her age, she had not gone to finishing school abroad, preferring to remain home.

A group of musicians from Barbados would have to be hired. Of course Mr. Callaghan could take care of that. On his frequent trips to the big island, he became acquainted with not only musicians, but it was rumoured that the middle-aged man during his sojourns abroad was involved in more than business ventures.

A date was set. The festivities would take place six months hence. Invitations were sent to all the plantations within a certain distance from the Callaghan home.

****

On the appointed day, the guests arrived amid great excitement. Coincidentally the arrival of the Governor on the island afforded the opportunity to extend an invitation to him and his entourage. No other occurrence of such import had ever taken place in the north country. It would certainly be the subject of conversation for many seasons to come.

Sheila, dressed in her new gown, took a place in a secluded alcove a little apart from the invited guests. Eithne, now six years old, sat beside her. She would be allowed to enjoy the festivities in honour of her older sister for an hour or two.

A sophisticated lady, vigorously fanning herself, raised her voice above the din of conversation. Within sight of Sheila, she looked her up and down and then tilting her head in a haughty manner commented, "So that's the governess we've all been hearing about. I wonder from whence she really comes. And," she continued, "you know, they say she doesn't even remember her name! What a tall story!"

Standing not too far off was the now infamous Edmund Hall. He studied Sheila's reactions or lack thereof, and concluded that she was really not concerned. She seemed above such trivia. She held her head high and conversed in cultured tones with the little girl at her side.

Then to the astonishment of those close by, Hall came to Sheila's defense, "Perhaps if you had been washed ashore and left for dead by the pounding waves, you too might have a lapse of memory, Madam."

Having delivered his rebuke, he turned on his heels and walked away. But for one second he glanced at Sheila, and in that instance their eyes met.

Like the touch of a butterfly's wing, a sensation soft but deep, thrilled her youthful heart. A slight blush suffused her pale cheeks as she lowered her head.

"See, see, Sheila," little Eithne distracted her. "See Anna. How beautiful she looks!"

"You're right. She is beautiful."

Anna had entered the room amid applause and was immediately presented to the Governor and his Lady. She wore a white silk gown, tight-fitting at the waist but with a full flowing skirt, upon which clusters of delicate pink rosettes were embroidered. Her shapely shoulders were bare. Her hair, caught up behind with a silver clasp, danced as she walked.

Many of the youth watching the scene were already smitten with the debutante. Anna would have no dearth of suitors.

Sheila also noted how Mr. Hall took stock of not only young Anna but also of many others in the room including herself. A surge of emotion swept over her. She saw herself as she might have been in a like situation in her father's castle with the cream of Ireland's young men in attendance, all of them vying for her favours.

She diverted her gaze as Anna moved away from the Governor. Then, as she looked around the room, she again saw Mr. Hall standing apart and alone; his gaze steady and determined as was he wont, directed not on the blushing debutante but upon herself. For the second time that evening, Sheila's heart fluttered. What on earth could he be thinking, she asked herself. Certainly, a lowly governess did not have much to offer a gentleman of his standing. He continued to watch her every move, yet Sheila kept her composure and recollected that although she was a governess in name, she was in reality his equal if not superior by birth and family tradition. She tried to ignore him and concentrated her attention on Eithne, who herself was attracting several older ladies as she danced to the soft tones of a flute playing in the distance.

****

Early the following afternoon as the household, with the exception of the servants and slaves, observed the two hour siesta, Sheila, unable to sleep, left her room and betook herself to the large sitting room. It had already been set to rights by the servants, so she counted on having no interruptions. She was finishing off a story for Eithne. The theme – the Irish Wolfhound. She had remembered the beautiful animals in her father's castle and wanted to inform her pupil of their special characteristics.

As she bent her head and pondered, the door was opened in a somewhat hasty manner. Looking up Sheila was surprised to find Mr. Edmund Hall standing there. A moment's hesitation before he decided to withdraw, "Beg your pardon, I had no idea that this room was occupied." Then on second thought, he took a few steps into the room and said, "May I ask why it is you do not follow the rules of your mistress and take a siesta?"

"Sir, I don't think that is any of your business," Sheila started to gather up her papers, intending to leave.

"Please, I forget myself. I'm accustomed to speaking to servants. Living alone, perhaps too long, has made me indifferent to…"

"Sir, you have no need to make excuses. If you wish to occupy this room, it is your right. You are a guest," Sheila moved toward the door.

"May I detain you a moment?" His voice had lost its edge. Almost a pleading tone evoked a feeling of compassion in Sheila's sensitive soul.

She faced him and looked into his dark brooding eyes.

"Please. Please be seated a moment longer. I would fain know something more about your past…if that is possible."

"To what purpose, Sir? Would you perhaps wish to hire me? But seeing that you have no children, I'm at a loss as to your reasons for doing so."

"Sheila."

Her name sounded like music as the word lingered on his lips. But Sheila was on her guard. She again sat down.

"I have been observing you. Of that you are aware, no doubt."

"Only too well," answered Sheila.

"You are not of the common folk. You are not merely a governess, of that I am sure," he drew nearer and then seated himself beside her. "Allow me, if you please, to tell you what I have concluded."

"It matters little what conclusions you have conceived, Sir. The facts remain. I'm not much better than a servant in this house and am likely to remain so for the rest of my life."

Edmund pressed forward, "If you will permit me to express my…" He paused as if choosing the right words.

"You are a very beautiful young woman. You have the poise and dignity of a well-bred educated lady. Your tone of voice is cultured and your speech impeccable." Again he paused.

Sheila's head was bent and her eyes had filled to overflowing. How long could she control herself?

"Shall I continue?" he asked.

"I think not, Sir. The hour grows late and I must attend the children," she arose without looking at him, and hurried from the room.

Edmund knew he had touched a sensitive chord. He knew she had a deep secret and he intended to uncover it ere he left Montserrat.

Chapter 12

"Love sought is good, but given unsought is better."
                    - Shakespeare

Word of a revolt on the Island of Barbados reached Montserrat. The Irish, it was taken for granted, were at the center of the rebellion. It was true several Irish servants and slaves had banded together and had run away from their masters. The exact number was not mentioned but it was large enough to cause much anxiety on the island. Blacks in large numbers had also taken flight and were causing mayhem on several of the larger plantations.

The names of three landowners were listed and the manner of their deaths described. They had been attacked with machetes, the blade used to cut the sugar cane. Two had been ambushed while traveling from their estates to the town of Plymouth. Dragged from their carriages, they were hacked to pieces; the third was killed in his own house.

It was further reported that several of the runaways had been captured, among them a number of women.

The Governor's task was clear. He would have to convene a court to deal with these miscreants as soon as he returned to Barbados.

Preparations were hastily made for the departure of the Governor and his party. They had spent three days with the Callaghan family. Early the following morning, they would bid adieu to their hosts.

Edmund had not laid eyes on Sheila since their encounter in the sitting room. Hence, he concluded that she had made it her business to avoid him. However, a man of his determination and purpose would not be easily deterred.

In accordance with the Governor's decision to cut short his stay in the Callaghan estate, a farewell gathering was hastily planned. The evening would begin with a sumptuous meal. There would be music and dancing following the dinner. And once again the young men would have ample opportunity to pay particular attention to Anna, especially Mr. Hall who hoped to obtain information concerning her governess – intimate details that only an admiring pupil would observe. Thus armed, he would then be able to make his next move.

It did not take long for the rumours to spread, "Mr. Hall is definitely interested in young Anna Callaghan."

Yes, it was quite obvious, even to Mistress Callaghan. Otherwise why would he spend time talking with her and quite openly seeking her company. However, were anyone to listen closely to the conversation between Edmund Hall and the young debutante, he or she would have drawn a very different conclusion.

"So you think Miss Sheila is from a good family, a society lady, as you call her?"

"Oh, yes, Sir, I'm sure of it. You, yourself, noted her manners, her speech. There is no doubt in my mind that her family were probably on their way to some estate on Barbados or Jamaica when the ship on which they were traveling was wrecked. She was the only one saved."

"Is that so," Mr. Hall was listening carefully.

"I'm glad she was saved," continued Anna. "She has been not only a superior mentor but a true friend to me."

"You really hold her in high esteem, then."

"Indeed, I do, Sir," continued Anna.

"You will excuse me, Anna. I'm much obliged to you for your frankness."

So saying, Edmund Hall arose and bowing, took a few steps backward. He then made his way to the section of the room where Sheila, accompanied by her charge, Eithne, was conversing with some other children.

The eyes of many in the room were upon him as tongues began to wag.

"He's looking for confirmation from the governess regarding Anna's accomplishments, I'll wager," words spoken by a matronly lady to Mistress Callaghan.

" 'Tis said he's worth more than £50,000," a lady who overheard the conversation commented. "That should mean something! It also brings up the question: wherefore being of a mature age, he's most certainly in his mid-twenties, has he not found a suitable bride in all of England? And, are his manners and behaviour too well-known in his native land that any well-bred young woman will have nothing to do with him?"

"Your point is well taken, Marsha," a fourth matron chimed in. "'Arrogant' and 'a brash youth' are the words most often used to describe him."

"Well, ladies, as yet he has not made his mind known to anyone and if what you say is true, you may be sure Mr. Callaghan and I, myself, will make doubly sure of his character before we consent to any contracts between our dear Anna and Mr. Edmund Hall."

Having delivered her final statement on the matter, Mistress Callaghan excused herself as she had other guests and other matters to attend.

Meantime, Edmund had seated himself in close proximity to Sheila and the children. Sitting on a rug at her feet, she had set the children a task. The child who drew the most exotic animal and who could make up the best story about that animal would have a rare treat.

Curious, Mr. Hall spoke to one of the children, "May I inquire as to what it is you are trying to accomplish, young man?"

The child, a little boy about seven or eight, lifted his head from his drawing, "Sir, I'm making a picture of Muchee, my make-believe animal. See, he has three legs and five arms! But I'm not finished. Miss Sheila says she will give a prize to the best story and drawing." The child resumed his work and instantly forgot Mr. Hall and the other adults who did not understand that he had a serious task to complete.

Hall seized the moment. "You seem to have a gift when it comes to the education and training of children, Miss Sheila."

"Thank you, Sir."

"In conversing with Miss Anna, I gathered that you were an excellent mentor. But more than that, the young lady assured me that you were a trusted and dear friend to her."

"Anna is a sweet and gentle girl, I should say lady, for as you can see she is no longer a girl," replied Sheila. "It was a joy and a privilege for me to have been entrusted with her education."

Now that Mr. Hall had succeeded in gaining her attention, he cautiously steered the conversation to the subject matter foremost in his mind.

"You are clever and astute, a woman of culture and learning. I have no doubt that you are from a good family. It is hardly fitting that a lady of your rank and talents should spend the rest of her life in such menial tasks and poor surroundings. I have the wherewithal to rescue you from this life…" he paused regarding her reaction intently.

Sheila glanced quickly around the room. As she had suspected, she was the center of attention.

She addressed Mr. Hall, "Sir, it is not seeming for a man of your status to be seen in the company of one such as I. At least that is the way of things on this island."

"I care little for such foibles, and I have observed it is also your position and stance regarding such unreasonable behaviour."

"You are a shrewd observer to have in such a short while plumbed the inner workings of my mind," she made as if she would rise, turning her attention to the children.

"Tarry a moment longer, please," there was a pleading in his voice of which she did not think him capable.

Sheila waited. Her gaze steady, she looked at him questioningly.

"Sheila," he hesitated.

She did not answer him, but continued to give him her full attention despite the mounting curiosity of those close by.

Edmund resumed, "I…I want you to be my wife."

At first she did not answer. Did she hear correctly? she asked herself.

One of the ladies standing close by heard the word 'wife' and immediately presumed that Hall was asking Sheila what she thought of Anna whom he wished to make his wife.

Word spread quickly. No doubt about it. The word wife was uttered. The excitement grew.

Edmund paid no attention to the consternation and curiosity his words had caused. Focused only on Sheila he seemed oblivious to all else. Anxious for her response, and seeing her doubt and hesitation, he lowered his voice and hastened to add, "I can give you all your heart desires. I have fallen in love with you. I did so the first time I laid eyes on you."

Sheila arose. Those within hearing distance must have caught some of his words. The whole room would be buzzing in a few minutes and she would be the laughing stock of the entire island within twenty-four hours. She was aware of the furtive glances. Blushing and embarrassed she became angry, "You do not know me, Sir. I'll hear no more."

She called to the children to follow her. They would finish their assignments in the schoolroom.

Before she turned her back on him, he addressed her once again, "You will not even consider my proposal?" His manner was abrupt.

"No, Sir." Then as she was about to leave, she continued, "And besides, I know nothing of you except that you are supposed to be a wealthy man. But that, Sir, does not tell a man's character."

Without another word, she turned and, followed by the children, left the room.

Her final words did not escape the ears of those standing around. Soon a new buzz of excitement filled the air.

Edmund Hall stood looking after her, seeming oblivious of the many eyes that were upon him.

Who was the woman, who, in the length and breadth of England would consider turning down an offer such as his? He was confused for the first time in his life. Certainly, she was unaware of his worth. But then he immediately recollected, she had mentioned that wealth did not a man's character prove. He chuckled at the irony of the situation. A woman of character, he had to confess, was rare. Ignoring the strangers surrounding him, all of whom were gossiping audibly, he promised himself that he would not take her words as final. And so as he too walked from the room, he planned accordingly.

He would not leave with the Governor's party the following morning. Confident that his position and a tidy sum would convince Mr. Callaghan of the need for some further discussion on a business transaction, Hall retired to the quiet of the sitting room down the hall to finalize his plans.

Chapter 13

"There in nothing half so sweet in life as love's young dream."

- *T. Moore*

The following morning before the Governor and his retinue departed, Edmund Hall approached Mr. Callaghan.

"I entreat your indulgence my good friend, I have a matter of great import which I would fain discuss with you at length. Seeing you have neither opportunity nor time at your disposal presently, I have taken the liberty to presume upon your hospitality for a few more days."

Thinking that Hall wished to discuss matters relating to the hand of his daughter, Anna, for he was not unmindful of the many rumours circulating regarding the matter, Callaghan eagerly embraced the idea, "You are most welcome, Sir, to stay as long as you wish. I'm honoured that you have chosen my humble home above all others."

At that juncture, the carriages to transport the Governor and many of the other guests were arriving. Callaghan excused himself and went to bid farewell to all who had so graciously attended his daughter's coming of age festivities.

Mistress Callaghan and Anna had already paid their respects when Mr. Hall made his way to the entrance. He bade the Governor and his wife adieu saying, "I'll join you in a few days, Sir. Perhaps then I may be able to persuade you to take a trip with me to the 'old sod.'"

108

"I'd like nothing better, my boy." Then *sotto voce*, "To feel young again, to enjoy the sights and sounds of London town, what could be more exhilarating!" Then he extended his hand and shook Edmund's vigorously.

Hall ignored the other parting guests and betook himself to the seclusion of the large sitting room which was deserted. He sat down to consider his next move.

****

Sheila had spent the morning with the younger children. Around noon, a light lunch was served in the dining room. She entered followed by Eithne and the three boys. The children quietly took their places at a side table. Having served the younger one, Sheila then seated herself beside them. A few guests still awaiting transportation to their homes were also present, while Mr. Hall had just served himself from the main, dishes laid out upon the sideboard, and had chosen to sit at a small table close to a window which overlooked a mango grove. It was obvious that he did not wish to be disturbed.

He glanced up from his plate just as Sheila happened to catch sight of him. He nodded, then bowed in her direction. His action was noted by those seated at the large main table.

Sheila lowered her eyes and self-consciously nibbled at her food. Then collecting herself, she gave her full attention to the children, correcting their table manners and their use of silverware.

No sooner had the last guest left the room when Edmund Hall approached, "Wherefore do you torment me? Must I endure at once too much and then again too little of your lovely face?"

Sheila blushed. The children were watching. "Sir," she responded, "I must see to the little ones. It's time for their siesta."

"Ah! Dare I hope that when sleep overtakes your charges, you will be able to spare me a few moments?" Edmund spoke in pleading tones.

"To what end, Sir?"

"Surely, you are not unaware of my feelings, my admiration, my love?"

"As I said before, you know me not. How then can you presume to say that you...? I must go. See, the children grow weary. I will see you later...in the sitting room."

Edmund's heart knocked against his ribs. But he would not show his emotion, particularly in light of the fact that the children were still present and listening to every word.

"Anon then. I'll be waiting."

They parted. Sheila was still apprehensive and wondered why she really accepted his invitation to meet with him again.

An hour later, Sheila went to her own room when she knew the children were all sound asleep and would, as was their wont, remain so for at least another hour. She found herself fixing her hair and setting her plain grey dress to rights. She patted her burning cheeks with a little powder, lest her heightened emotions be observed by Mr. Edmund Hall. He was persistent. Had he really postponed his departure on her account, or was his motive some business venture with Mr. Callaghan, as she had heard the housekeeper report. These and many other questions she asked herself as she descended to the formal living room.

Upon opening the door, she found Mr. Hall already seated in an armchair with a book in his hand. He was flipping through the pages but with care, lest the crumbling tome disintegrate.

He arose as she came forward, "You honour me, Miss Sheila. Please be seated." He already had set a chair close to his own.

Sheila sat down rather demurely, placing her hands over one another on her lap and waited for him to speak again.

"I will come to the point and be quite frank with you. I did not postpone my departure in order to discuss business with Mr. Callaghan as you have, no doubt, been told. My only excuse, my only reason, is precisely to have this conversation with you."

"Sir!" Sheila was taken aback. "You should not on my account have delayed your departure. You already know my answer. Why do you persist?"

"Because, my dear, it is not in my nature to give up so easily. I am of the persistent type. And besides I know my own heart and it will not allow me to act contrariwise."

Sheila remained silent, observing his every movement – the inflection of his voice, the facial expressions, the gestures his hand made. He was indeed alive, more passionate and animated than she had ever seen him. His slow, aloof and calculating manner had vanished completely; he was a man invigorated, vibrant. His eyes sparkled, his speech was soft, even tender, his deportment though still reserved, had lost the haughty standoffish element that had been his up to this point.

"I have not slept. I have not had five minutes ease since I laid eyes on you, Miss Sheila. It's as if you had cast a spell upon me." Then to lighten the tension between them he added, "Are you one of those fairy folk then? A sprite from an other world sent to torture the hearts of young men?"

Sheila found her tongue, "I wager, Mr. Hall, you are like most young men, heartless. I have observed how men act and the experience is not to my liking."

"I'm sorry you have had such experiences. But I assure you all young men do not fall into such a category."

"Of that I am pleased to hear," Sheila still maintained her composure and held her demure posture.

"Allow me, sweet lady, to again affirm my undying love for you. I beg your indulgence and plead with you to reconsider my offer, my proposal."

"Sir, I reiterate what I have previously said. How can you, a man of substance, a man well known in your native land whom, I venture to say, has the pick of all the young ladies of wealth and status in that country, ask me, a lowly governess, to become your wife?"

"The simple answer, in fact the only answer, is because I have fallen in love with you. Your reply, 'You do not know me,' is of little concern to me."

"It seems to me now, Sir, that you really think you are in love with me. I do not doubt the sincerity of your words at this moment...but..."

"Again, I do not know you, is this your reply?" he asked.

"I'm afraid so," Sheila answered.

"Well, then let's take care of that barrier that stands between us. Why don't you tell me, as best you can, who you are and from whence you came."

Sheila trembled, then blushed and became pensive a moment. She looked up and into Edmund's eyes. She saw there a tenderness, and an encouraging, pleading expression which seemed to draw forth the words she swore she never would utter.

"I will not lie to you, Sir. But I would plead with you that when you have heard my tale and then probably changed your mind in my regard, you will, at least, hold my secret within your heart and allow me to hold my position here in this house where I'm respected and appreciated," Sheila waited for Edmund's reply.

"You have my word on that. Even were you a monster from the deep, which I know you are not," here he smiled, "your secret will be forever buried in the depths of my soul never again to know the light of day."

"Then Sir I will bare mine."

Sheila told her story and the tears came fast and furious as she painted a picture of her beloved family and her native land.

At that juncture, Edmund arose and taking her in his arms, gently placed a kiss on her moist brow. After a moment or two when she again composed herself he reiterated the sentiments which flowed from a heart welling up with deep emotions, "You have suffered enough Sheila McCarthy. It is time for us to go home."

Home, the very word she had not dared to utter for the past eight years! Was she dreaming? Was this young man not only her future husband but her saviour? Her heart could scarce bear the happiness. Then she considered her situation again.

"What of my obligations here and the children?" she thought aloud.

"No obstacle exists that cannot be overcome. No hurdle so high that it cannot be scaled. Where there is determination and will to prevail, all is possible, my lovely Sheila."

Together they formulated a plan whereby no one would be inconvenienced by Sheila's departure. He would return to

Barbados, find there an Irishwoman with suitable education and background, and rescue her from the tortures of the sugarcane plantation. He would outfit her with whatever she needed to appear respectable and return with her to the Callaghan estate as soon as he could.

In the meantime no one should be apprised of their intentions. Edmund took Sheila in his arms again and before they parted, she received her first real kiss.

Mr. Hall tarried in the Callaghan household for one more day. He saw Sheila briefly but spent several hours conversing with Mistress Callaghan. Then a bargain was made with the master of the plantation. He offered him a better price for his sugar were he to deal with him directly than with his present buyer. The matter of Anna's future was not discussed. And so Mr. Callaghan concluded that Hall's sole purpose in remaining behind when the rest of the Governor's party left was solely to profit from this business venture with himself.

What Hall discussed with the lady of the house was not divulged. So it was that Mr. Edmund Hall departed the island of Montserrat.

Chapter 14

"Hope is brightest when it dawns from fear."
- *Walter Scott*

A month…. two months, went by, and not a word about Mr. Hall's activities or whether he was still living on the island of Barbados reached Montserrat.

The hope Sheila carried deep within her heart, of one day having a better life and someone to love and care for her began to wane. Had she been led astray by the arrogant Mr. Hall after all? Was she one of the many she had heard whispered about that he had deceived? Was he laughing now at his easy conquest? Questions such as these kept hammering at her brain night and day for the past month.

She lay tossing on her hard bed one night unable to sleep. The tropical moon, full, round, golden bright had flooded her tiny room with its pale light. She left her bed and, clad only in her white nightgown, went to the window. Spreading her arms wide, she lifted her sweet voice in a heart-wrenching plea:

La Luna

Oh, silver moon so clear so bright
Please guide my love to me this night.
Tell him I wait, I sigh and pray
The words he spoke were not in play.
His ship I see not on the tide.
No word, no message reached his bride.
Oh, gentle moon please light his way

Ere hope is dead and dreams decay.

Her song ended in a heartfelt sob as she slumped to the floor.

Below her, Anna was awakened by the plaintive melody. She did not understand the words, however, as Sheila had used her native language which spoke so much more intensely to her aching heart.

But hearing the thud, she became alarmed and hastily leaving her bed, she went straight to Sheila's room. Getting no answer to her frantic knocking, she opened the door only to find Sheila collapsed on the floor. Immediately she tried to lift her back to her bed. The movement caused Sheila to moan and open her eyes.

"Where am I? What has happened?" she asked.

"You fainted, I think," answered Anna. "Stay a moment and then I'll help you get back into bed. I'll fetch Mama, she'll know what to do."

"Oh no, no. Just a drink of water – I'll be all right. No need to disturb your mother." Sheila thought a moment. "Perhaps I have not been eating enough. I'll sleep now, thank you, Anna," she continued after having taken a few sips of water.

"If you are quite sure. I'll leave and allow you to get some sleep," Anna did not mention the sad lament she had heard earlier.

"Yes, I'm sure, dear Anna. Thank you again for coming to my assistance. Have a good night yourself."

Anna left closing the door gently behind her.

Sheila settled into a deep sleep and did not wake until the noisy children woke her the next morning.

Her morning duties in the schoolroom having been accomplished, as was her wont Sheila took the younger children to the dining room for their midday meal. They had scarce begun to eat when a servant hurriedly entered the room and went directly to Mistress Callaghan at the main table. The Master of the house was away on business and had been absent for a week or more.

"A gentleman, Mistress, has just arrived and wishes to be presented to you. May I ask him to step in here?"

"Why, certainly. He will no doubt have need of something to eat. You might check the sideboard to see if there are sufficient meats and vegetables."

The servant left but soon returned accompanied by Mr. Edmund Hall. He was none the worse for his journey. On the contrary, he seemed fit and full of energy.

Sheila, on the other hand, was visibly shaken. She turned pale and her hands shook as she tried to serve the children. She dared not look at him lest she repeat the episode of the previous night.

Mr. Hall seated himself beside Mistress Callaghan at the main table. Soon a maidservant served him and the butler poured some fine wine. He was pleasant enquiring about the family. Anna was now seated opposite him and he bowed politely to her and remarked, "You grow more beautiful, Mademoiselle. Even a few months makes a difference in the life of a young woman, I wager."

"Thank you, Sir," replied Anna, blushing slightly.

The conversation then turned to more serious matters – his meeting in Barbados with Mr. Callaghan and the conducting of some business. Sheila paid attention and tried hard to hide her trepidation by being over-attentive to the children.

Soon Mrs. Callaghan and Mr. Hall arose. It seemed they would adjourn to the sitting room for further discussions.

As he passed close to Sheila's table, he stopped briefly and bowed to her. As he ran his fingers through Eithne's hair in friendly fashion teasing the child, he whispered to Sheila, "Not too long more. Be ready." Then he passed on.

Sheila could hardly contain herself. Her heartbeat quickened, her stomach heaved and a cold perspiration drenched her brow.

As soon as the door closed, she gathered the children together and they all repaired to the schoolroom and thence to their beds for it was siesta time.

This gave Sheila time to ponder Edmund's words, 'Not too much longer. Be ready.' Did he mean to take her that night or would she wait and wait, as she had already done, for another two or three months? It was impossible for her to fathom. Yet, what if he intended that she leave with him that evening? No, it would certainly be morning. Where would they go once nightfall was upon them? These questions and a hundred others crowded her mind. She finally decided that the best course of action for her was not to act. She would wait for further word before doing anything. Why alert the servants or the children, in fact the whole household, unnecessarily?

In the meantime, Edmund and Madam Callaghan were sequestered in the living room. No doubt he was broaching the subject, the real purpose of his unexpected visit.

****

Seated in an armchair Madam Callaghan was eager to hear about what Mr. Hall had to tell her. Many thoughts ran through her mind, uppermost the idea that perhaps Anna might be the reason for his coming. She waited for Mr. Hall to speak.

Having delivered a letter from her husband and assuring her that he was well and would probably be home in a day or two, he then proceeded with great care to address the subject uppermost in his mind.

"Mistress Callaghan, your husband and I have had lengthy discussions as you well know regarding several business transactions, one in particular appertains to your governess, Miss Sheila," he was careful not to mention her last name.

"Miss Sheila!" Mistress Callaghan was obviously shocked. "I don't understand. What…what business transaction could you possibly have regarding the children's governess?"

"My dear Mistress Callaghan, my words, I fear, were badly chosen. I did not mean to imply that the conversations I had regarding Miss Sheila were business discussions. To be quite frank with you, and to put the matter as bluntly as I can, dear lady, I'm in love with…"

"You mean to tell me that a man of your status and influence has a mind to marry a lowly governess? What of Anna then? I thought…"

"Yes, Madam, that is the…"

"And apart from dear Anna," Madam Callaghan was not listening. Her mind was in a whirl. What would her neighbours think! The island would make fine sport of the whole affair. Then she thought of her children, "My children, what may I ask, are they to do without a governess? I'm quite appalled by the whole situation."

"Mistress Callaghan," said Mr. Hall, "your husband and I have made provision. By tomorrow morning Miss Una

O'Brien, a well-educated and refined young woman will arrive here. I do hope she will meet with your approval."

"Huh, indeed I'm not so sure that in matters relating to children's needs a man can make the correct decisions," Mistress Callaghan said, then arose.

Then as if a totally new and unexpected idea had just struck her, she blurted, "And is Miss Sheila aware of the inconvenience she is causing? Have you, Sir, even consulted her regarding these matters? I cannot imagine, but then what can one expect from a…I can only blame myself for employing her in the first place."

She mused a second. Then began again, "And after all I've done for her, deceiving miserable wretch. Not one word did she say, yet knowing all the time that she was the object of your desire and not my Anna. It's a disgusting business." Mistress Callaghan abruptly turned toward the door, leaving Mr. Hall standing with a puzzled look in his dark brown eyes. He had undoubtedly offended the lady, but why or how he had not the slightest idea.

"Oh well," he was about to sit down again when Mistress Callaghan turned to face him just as she was about to open the door.

"Perhaps I've been a little too hasty," she said. "Before consulting Mr. Callaghan, had you made known your plans to Miss Sheila? How much of all you have told me was she aware?"

"Frankly, dear lady, very little. I did ask her to be my wife before I left but her answer was vague and I would hardly say enthusiastic."

Mistress Callaghan seemed to accept his answer as she quickly followed with a proposal of her own: "Anna is still very young, as you know, Sir. She has several years in which to find a suitable partner. Yet, in this small island there are few ideal men from whom to choose. Most of the young men go abroad to be educated and naturally find wives more to their liking and…shall we say, standards, in foreign countries. Now Mr. Hall," she hurried on, "if you could see your way, in due time of course, to invite Anna, say to spend a few months with you and your wife…"

"Mistress Callaghan, what a brilliant idea! Most certainly, Sheila and I would be honoured to have such a sweet and lovely young lady in our home for whatever time," he paused as if considering a sudden inspiration hitherto undreamt of. "In fact, I know how highly Sheila thinks of Anna. It would be a consolation I'm sure, for her to have a close friend in a strange new land. Give us six months to settle into our new married life which I hope will occur as soon as we return to England. Then I will arrange for Anna's journey to our home where we will introduce her to the very best families I know."

"Oh, Mr. Hall you are so kind. As I have so often told my friends, I believed you to be a man of rectitude and unblemished character," Mistress Callaghan's attitude had changed completely. From that moment she could not do enough for Mr. Hall and Sheila.

Part III

Boston

Charles River

Harbor

New Boston

Old Boston

Boston
Common

Public
Garden

New Boston

Fort Point
Channel

New Boston

Boston - 1600's

Chapter 15

Colonial America

England in the 1620s had to contend with religious and political turmoil. In 1629 the struggle between the monarchy and the Parliament reached its climax. It was then that Charles I disbanded his rivals (among whom were the Puritans and the Pilgrims) and took complete charge for the next eleven years.

In 1628, a group of Puritan businessmen banded together to form the Governor and Company of Massachusetts Bay. This they conceived would be a profit-making enterprise in the New World. They received a land grant from the Council of New England which gave them rights to the area between the Charles and Merrimack Rivers as well as westward to the Pacific Ocean. Voyages were made in 1628 and 1629 resulting in the establishment of the colony of Cape Ann and later in Salem.

Eventually, the company which had started as a trading venture became an organized group dominated by stalwart Puritans who had a religious agenda.

In the new colony only fellow believers were eligible for political power. Therefore, they in essence created a theocracy.

Governor John Whinthrop controlled the arrival of around 1000 colonists in 1630. These new settlers initially made Salem their home base, but soon moved to a more advantageous location on the Shawmut Peninsula of Massachusetts Bay (later called Boston.)

The settlers endured great hardships and almost 200 died the first year, while in the spring of 1631 a like number returned to England. However, improvements, though gradual, led to an increase in the number of colonists, and over the following 10 years as many as 20,000 people arrived.

In the succeeding years, new settlements were established in such places as Lexington, Concord, Charlestown and others. The Puritan influence was felt throughout the entire community. They held the belief that all mankind deserved eternal damnation but only a few through the mercy of God were granted salvation – these were the Elect. They also believed that being God's chosen people they were bound by a covenant to enforce God's laws in society. Hence, the actions and activities of one's neighbour were of continual interest.

With such a mindset, it is easy to understand why it did not take long to conceive the happenings for which the town of Salem, in particular, became infamous.

Boston – Early History

Founded in 1630, Boston was visited by several explorers before that time, among them John Cabot, who with his three sons set sail from England in 1497 to establish Henry VII's right to possession of what we now call New England. Another explorer was Captain John Smith, who in 1614 sailed along the North American shoreline and made a map of the area.

The Pilgrims landed in 1620 and it was they who established the first permanent settlement at Plymouth on

Massachusetts Bay about forty miles south of present day Boston.

The old Indian name for the town was Shawmut, meaning 'Living Waters.' According to the author, Marjorie Drake Ross: "The original Shawmut was a small, wide peninsula connected to the mainland by a very narrow neck. There were about seven hundred and eighty-three acres indented deeply by coves and almost surrounded by water. In the center were three hills: Trimountain, Copp's Hill and Fort Hill. The Trimountain had three peaks known as Pemberton, Beacon, and Mount Vernon."

The first enduring settlement in the Boston area is attributed to Sir Ferdinando Gorges, an intimate friend of Sir Walter Raleigh. John Smith had touched the shores of New England and even ventured into Boston Harbour before Gorges and even Miles Standish had come from Plymouth to trade with the Indians. Thomas Weston had even set up a trading-post in Weymouth but it was Gorges and his son Robert who firmly planted the standard of England on America's shores even though the Cabots had come to this land a century and a quarter before.

The next in line to leave his mark on New England was Captain John Smith. That region, as well as Virginia, owe much to this man. He writes as follows: "When I went first to the North part of Virginia, (in 1614) where the Westerly colony (of 1607) had been planted, which had dissolved itself within a yeare, there was not one Christian in all the land. The country was then reputed a most rockie, barren, desolate desert; but the good return I brought from thence, with the maps and relations I made of the country, which I made so manifest, some of them did believe me, and they were well embraced, both by the Londoners and

---

the Westerlings, for when I had promised to undertake it, thinking to have joyned them all together..."

In choosing a name for the new settlement, the community was unanimous. It was called after the city in the Old World, St. Botolph's town in Lincolnshire, England. And Governor Winthrop presiding on September 17th, 1630 stated: "That Trimountain shall be called Boston."

The name St. Botolph is attributed to a pious Saxon monk of the seventh century, who is believed to have founded the original town in Lincolnshire. The name is derived from the words Bot-hold or Boat-help – as the monk, we are told, rendered service to sailors. The steeple of the church was originally designed to be a guide to those at sea, and it was in remembrance of the beacon in St. Botolph's tower that the Court of Assistants met in the new Boston and passed the resolutions on March 4, 1634: "It is ordered that there shalbe forth with a beacon sett on the Centry hill at Boston to give notice to the Country of any danger, and that there shalbe a ward of one person kept there from the first of April to the last of September; and that upon the discovery of any danger the beacon shalbe fired, an allarum given, as also messengers presently sent by that town where the danger is discov'red to all other towns within this jurisdiction."

But these influences on Boston were not the only ones. The old St. Botolph's town with its winding streets played a large part in the layout of the new Boston. Hawthorne suggests, "It's crooked streets and narrow lanes reminded me much of Hanover street, Ann street, and other portions of our American Boston. It is not unreasonable to suppose that the local habits and recollections of the first settlers may have had some influence on the physical character of the streets and houses in the New England metropolis; at any rate here is a similar intricacy of bewildering lanes and a number of old peaked and projecting-storied dwellings, such as I used to see there in my boyish days. It is singular what a home feeling and sense of kindred I derived from this hereditary connection and fancied physiognomical resemblance between the old town and its well-grown daughter."[13]

13   Crawford, Mary Caroline. Old Boston in Colonial Days. L.C. Page & Company, Boston. 1908. p. 45.

Chapter 16

"Interwoven is the love of liberty with every ligament of the heart."

- *Washington*

Anne 'Goody' Glover was born in Ireland in a little village in the county of Clare. Her parents were in possession of a small parcel of land when 'Goody' was young but like most of the Catholics of their time when Cromwell tried to rid the land of their kind, they were left destitute. When they refused to leave their home, they were quickly dispatched to the next life: the order being 'To Hell or to Connaught.'

'Goody,' a young girl of about sixteen, strong and healthy, was in the eyes of the English soldiers more valuable than her parents or for that matter her baby brother. He was also put to the sword following the orders of Sir Charles Coote in charge of the forces in Connaught whose command was to "kill the nits and you will have no lice." 'Goody' on the other hand would fetch a goodly sum in the English slave market.

Ann Glover was known to her friends and childhood companions as 'Goody.' Why such a name or nickname was given to her is conjecture. She never revealed the reason and those who were curious had only one answer. It was said that she was a mild-mannered child, always attentive to the wishes of her parents and elders. The local children had a penchant for nicknames. Each one of them having his or her own peculiar character and mannerisms was duly renamed by their peers as they thought fit. There was 'hop along Cassidy,' a boy who had a slight limp and 'mousey' Nelly, a timid girl, and Peig 'Rua,' red-haired Peg. Then there was Taig *'a da taobh,'* the person not to be trusted, and *'An ciotog,'* the left-handed one. A virtuous and obedient child was a 'goody-goody' so that cognomen naturally suited Ann. She would carry the name for the rest of her life.

Having been sold as a slave, she arrived in Barbados in the late 1650s and remained there for the next ten years. Her husband, an Irishman whom she met on the plantation, died while still young. "Beaten to death he was, all because he would not renounce his Catholic faith," were the words of 'Goody' as she made known the facts to her daughter, Moira; the child he never knew.

Moira favoured her mother in looks and temperament. Fair-skinned, her hair a chestnut colour fell in ringlets to her waist. She had blue-grey eyes and her pale cheeks showed little dimples when she smiled. She was her mother's pride and joy, a child pliable and easy to raise in the ways of God.

****

One day on board *The Hanna* was much the same as the next as far as 'Goody' and her daughter were concerned. Their lives were continuously occupied with planning and preparing food for the captain and his crew. As long as they could please their new master, they felt they were safe aboard the trading vessel as it made its way northward. The drudgery among the pots and pans was nothing compared with what they had escaped in the sugarcane fields of Barbados. Only the temper of the weather disturbed their monotonous existence.

But they were thankful to be 'free.' Free from the tropical sun, the lash and the grinding toil in the sugar plantation. One day, they promised themselves, real freedom would be theirs. They would be free to earn an honest living, and they would be free to practice their religion, for they were thoroughly grounded in their Catholic faith. Perhaps they might even have a home of their own: a place where they would be safe and secure. 'Goody' dreamed and dreamed. She might even live to see her grandchildren.

"All in God's good time," she often said. "If only my Rory were alive." And then she would quickly add: "Ah, but he's in a better place and lookin' down on us he is and smilin' and watchin' over us. God bless him."

They had no idea where they were in relation to land. Nor did they have any notion as to how long it would take to arrive at their destination or what fate awaited them when finally they did land at a place called Boston.

It was late in the evening when the watch alerted the captain and crew with the words: "Cape Cod, Ahoy!"

A strong breeze blew from the northeast and the captain, sensing unfavourable weather and not wishing to have to return to Rhode Island, set the sails.

By nightfall, *The Hanna* had gained the relative protection of the Bay. The captain gave the order to drop anchor. They would spend the night there and proceed northwest at the morning's first light, their destination the settlement of Boston.

The excitement among the members of the crew was contagious and soon 'Goody' and her daughter, Moira, were infected by the 'bug.'

"This Boston town must be quite the place!" 'Goody' spoke in subdued tones, "With God's help we'll find a means of surviving and making a better life for ourselves, daughter."

"Aye, Mother, I do hope so."

Then in a playful turn, still speaking in the Gaelic tongue, she whispered, "Maybe you'll be findin' a fine young man for yourself. Let him be Irish, though, and Catholic."

"Oh, Mother, your plans reach to heaven itself."

By midday, the ship had reached the entrance to the harbour. A rolling sea caused considerable turbulence below deck. Pots and pans were flung hither and yon. But 'Goody' and her daughter no longer feared the terrors of the sea. They sat quietly in a safe place and waited for the waves to push the vessel into calmer waters. By late afternoon the ship dropped anchor in the bay. The town lay directly before them. 'Goody' had left everything in order in the galley, had gathered herself and a small portion of food together and mounted the steep ladder to the deck. She and her daughter bade farewell to the captain before they stepped onto the gangway to freedom.

They walked across the large dock constructed of wooden piers. Ahead atop a high hill stood the lighthouse which guided so many vessels to the safety of the port. The spot soon became known as Beacon Hill. Looking around they were quite surprised to find that they were now in a fairly large city. Several trading companies had their businesses along the wharf. They noticed that the houses were made of thin cedar shingles nailed to the frames. Some did have bricks or other solid material around the windows and doors.

"We must hasten afore the darkness comes. Somewhere to sleep, *alanah*, is what we must find."

They walked further. Several women and children passed by hurrying along as if they too wished to get home before dark. 'Goody' stopped a woman who looked more like herself. Not too well-dressed, she appeared worried and exhausted.

"Beg pardon, Mam. We are strangers here. Could you direct me to some household in need of a cook or washerwoman?"

The woman looked at the two a moment. "'Tis hard to come by honest work in this town. So many black, aye, even white slaves employed these days. No room for the likes of us," she paused. "But ye might try in that house yonder." She pointed to a large building set back from the street and enclosed behind iron gates.

"That's Mr. John Goodwin's home. He has several children – a large family. He's not the kind to keep slaves. Ye might be lucky. I'd 'a gone there meself for work exceptin' I caught the fever. Aye, then my strength was gone. Now I can only beg for a livin'." She hesitated, seeing how ill-clad the strangers were. Then she added, "Perhaps ye might have a penny to spare?"

"Sorry Mam, we don't have a farthing between us," answered 'Goody.'

"I didn't think so," she mumbled to herself, "Then I'll be sayin' good luck to ye." Without another word, the beggar woman walked away.

'Goody' took her daughter's hand and together they approached the Goodwin property.

Knowing better than to knock on the front door, they made their way to the back. It was now dark and turning cold. Moira in her thin cotton dress was shivering.

'Goody' knocked on the door. For a few moments all was silent. Then a woman's voice from within called, "Who's there?"

"My daughter and I seek employment if that be possible. I'm a good cook an'..."

Before she had finished speaking, the door was flung open and a rather stout woman in her early forties holding a lantern peered into the darkness at the two.

"Where ya come from?" she asked.

"We just came off the boat a while ago. We were told that you might be in need of a good cook or a..."

"Come in. You may very well be the person I'm lookin' for," the woman at the door interjected.

As soon as she had shut the door and placed the lantern on a table close by, she again turned to face the newcomers.

"My name is Kate Quinn. I'm the housekeeper, and manage such business for the household. We had to let the washerwoman go last week and have been lookin' for a suitable woman since. Your name is?"

"My name is Ann 'Goody' Glover and this is my daughter, Moira. We would be willing to have the position," she hesitated. "That is, of course, depending on the conditions."

"Of course. But since it is dark now and rather difficult to show you the quarters and scrub-house, perhaps you could come back in the morning?"

'Goody' waited without saying a word.

Kate was an Irishwoman, who had come to Boston as an indentured servant some twenty years previous. Now in her late forties, she was a free employee working for wages and in a responsible position. A gentile woman, she was respected by all in the household.

"Forgive me, you did say you just came from the ship. I forgot for the moment. You don't have a place to stay and if I am to employ you in the morning you might as well be introduced to your room. I'm sorry, only one room has been allotted to the washerwoman, so you're daughter will have to share. I'll allow her to stay with you until she gets to know the town. Eventually, she will have to find her own way however.

"God bless you, Kate Quinn. This is right decent of you." Tears welled up and rolled down 'Goody's face. She was tired and hungry. "Would I be troublin' you too much if my daughter and I could share a wee cup of water and a slice of bread?"

"Sure, of course. You'll have a hot supper. 'Tis the least I can do for such a fine woman from the 'old sod.'"

Kate showed them a room at the back of the house. It had a bed, a nightstand with a washbasin and jug, a chair and an old cedar chest. It was a luxurious abode as far as 'Goody' was concerned. A real bed after almost twenty years of sleeping on the hard ground in all kinds of weather. For the ground on which she had slept for the most part was damp, if not soaking wet. The flimsy hut she called home rarely kept the tropical rains without in the wet season. Now she had a solid roof over her head, a room that was dry and comfortable. What more could she hope for?

Chapter 17

"Creeds grow so thick along the way their boughs hide God."

- *Lizette Woodworth Reese*

The next few years were, by and large, uneventful, almost monotonous, for Ann and her daughter with the exception of Moira's marriage and an increase in the number of children in the Goodwin family, five children in fact. Happy, carefree, and boisterous, they clamoured for attention and ran 'wild' around the large house from morning to night. They ran up and down the stairs, slid on the banisters, tumbled in the hallways, banged doors and in general made perfect nuisances of themselves as far as the servants were concerned. The mistress of the house was ill-equipped to deal with them, she being in poor health and confined to her bed for long periods.

Eventually, a governess was employed – I should say many governesses were employed – for no governess spent more than six months trying to control the unruly bunch until Harriet Baldwin took up residence in the Goodwin home.

Of course the true reason for the frequent turnover of instructors in his house was completely unknown to Mr. John Goodwin, who spent most of his waking hours in his office, and when he did darken his front door, the little ones were already in bed and the older children on their very best behaviour.

Miss Harriet was an English woman of the Puritan faith, she spared not the rod nor the lash of her tongue. Her favourite saying, as one can well imagine, was: "Spare the rod and spoil the child." So it was by dint of hammering home the tenets of her persuasion that she eventually succeeded in taming the noisy brood. With a leather strap, Harriet Baldwin, then in her late forties, grey-haired and wrinkled, beat the desk in front of her with a loud bang.

The children, unaccustomed to such extreme behaviour, were at once quieted. Then in a forceful manner and with a high-pitched voice, she delivered her warnings.

"You force the Hand of God. Know ye not what the Lord God will do to unruly and disobedient children? Well, let me tell you."

A lecture on the wrath of God and the consequences of their incorrigible behaviour followed. Soon the servants noticed the change. The exuberant, happy children of yesterday had become gloomy and pensive. Unable to expend their excess energy as normal healthy children, they moped about looking for faults in themselves and others. But the household was a much quieter place. The servants were able to go about their chores unimpeded and the 'Lady' of the house was allowed to rest and thereby gained a little more strength and health.

But before we continue with the Goodwin family's story, we must digress to fill in the highlights of Ann's life to this point.

Moira had grown into a strong if not beautiful young woman. Plain of face, she yet possessed a certain charm that attracted strangers to her. The dimples of childhood remained and grew larger as she matured, making her smile her greatest asset.

On her day off, which was usually Sunday, she was wont to spend time on the beach or near the waterfront, especially in the summer. It was in this way that she had the opportunity to get to know people of her own age.

Unbeknownst to her, for many months, a young man in his mid-twenties had been watching and taking stock of her every move. His name was Brian O'Riordan. A strong youth, he was the son of Dermud, a dock worker who had come to America from Ireland as a young indentured servant. Having served his time as a farmhand, he eventually obtained his freedom and went to work as a boat loader. In time he married an Irish woman and together they had three sons. Brian was the oldest and most like his father, so it was only natural for him to follow the 'old man' to the waterfront to seek employment there also.

As the trading vessels came and went with the tides, there was little free time for the dock workers. But Brian could not help noticing the pretty girls as they strolled along the wharf, among them the slender Moira Glover. "The girl with the beautiful smile," was Brian's description of her.

Brian was Catholic, but like the rest of his kind, unable to practice his religion. No Catholic priest was allowed to preach or hold service within the Puritan Community. Many who had come from Ireland in the 40's and 50's had lost their religion in such surroundings or converted to the Puritan creed. Brian, like Moira and her mother, were determined however to hold steadfast to their Catholic faith.

Toward the end of summer in the year 1686, one Sunday while most of her friends were attending church service, Moira sat all alone on a bench near the waterfront. She was watching the rippling tide-waters play among the rocks and, absorbed in her own thoughts, was startled when suddenly a man's voice, clear and magical, broke through the still morning air. The light tenor voice was that of Brian O'Riordan, and his intention soon became obvious.

As he drew near, Moira noticed he had a small bouquet of red roses in his hand. And the song he sang was a fitting choice:

> See, I have brought you a gift of sweet
>   blossoms,
> Tender and fair and all gleaming with dew,
> Take them and keep them, these flowers of
>   the summer,
> Wonderful, beautiful roses for you!
>
> Life be for you a garden of sunshine,
> Clouds never darken, your skies all be blue,
> God give you happiness, love and His
>   blessing,
> These shall be beautiful roses for you!

Walking up to where Moira was sitting, Brian doffed his woolen cap and introduced himself.

"Brian O'Riordan is the name," and without hesitation he continued, "I've seen you here off an' on for the past few months with your friends an' I've been wonderin' who you are."

"Well, Brian O'Riordan," answered Moira, "I'm Moira Glover and I'm happy to make your acquaintance."

"May I sit awhile then?"

"Sure," she answered and made room for him on the bench.

They talked together for about an hour; then when the worshippers started to wend their way homeward, Moira thought it appropriate that she should do so also. In such a society rumours quickly spread, and one could lose one's good name overnight.

"Perhaps we could meet again next Sunday," he suggested.

"I'd like that," Moira answered. "Same place, same time?"

"That would suit me fine. I really enjoyed our time together, Moira." His voice was soft and tender.

"Well, bye then for now. Or, as they say in Ireland, *Sláin leat.*"

"*Sláin leat is go n'eirig do boither leat, a cailin deas dilis,*"[14] came the eager response. Then with a wave of his hand he waited until she was quite a distance away. He picked his well-worn cap off the bench, and donning it quickly he set off for his own home quite pleased with himself.

Moira, flushed and excited, flung the door open and ran into the kitchen of the Goodwin residence. Bent on telling her mother the good news, she ran straight into the housekeeper, Una Quinn.

"What have we here, now? An admirer, is it?" she asked, almost as excited as Moira herself.

"Maybe," Moira wasn't going to admit the obvious just yet. "Where is mother?"

"Don't know. Maybe she's takin' a little walk. She deserves a free moment to herself now an' again. Anyway I haven't seen her all mornin' and come to think of it, nor yerself either," Una answered with a twinkle in her eye.

---

14   "Goodbye and may the road rise up before you, my pretty charming girl."

"But those gorgeous flowers deserve some water otherwise they won't live till yer Ma gets back. How about a vase?"

"Oh, yes. That's a good idea," Moira still excited tried to hide her trembling hands.

While they were arranging the flowers, Ann walked in. There was a moment of silence, then Una spoke.

"I think Moira has something important to tell you, Ann."

"Oh! An' what would that be?"

Again silence, for Moira did not want to divulge her secret to the whole world. At least not as yet.

"Ooh! So that's it then." Ann caught the wink in Una's eye and the fresh roses hadn't escaped her either. A broad smile lit up her tired face.

"Ah, why not," Moira, as if answering for her own hesitation and embarrassment and realizing that there was no other way out started to talk, "well…"

"Look at the beautiful flowers someone, an admirer, no doubt, gave her this morning," Una interrupted intending to encourage.

"Ooh, so that's it." Ann was beaming. "Well out with it. Let's know the whole story."

"An' let's all have a cup o' tea an' a piece o' pie as well."

And so the encounter with Brian O'Riordan was vividly described. The older women, exchanging glances now and then, were well pleased with what they consi-dered was the beginning of a real romance.

Six months later, their predictions were fulfilled. Moira and Brian were wed in a simple ceremony. They exchanged their vows before their parents in the O'Riordan home.

There was no Catholic priest to officiate and they would not have any other minister to bless their union.

It was a happy occasion for all concerned. A few days later, Moira gathered her belongings together and moved to the O'Riordan home, but she still continued to work for the Goodwin family.

In due time, a baby girl was born and was baptized by her father, who named her Anna Kathleen in honour of both grandmothers.

The joy and happiness the tiny creature brought into the families was beyond expression. She grew daily in health and beauty beloved by all but particularly by her grandmother Ann, who could not do enough for her.

Chapter 18

"He who commits injustice is ever made more wretched than he who suffers it."

- *Plato*

Winter had come early to the region in the year 1687. Bitter blasts of icy cold rain and wind plagued the Boston area for days on end. Then suddenly, the temperature dropped and overnight the snow came. Morning's light saw a powdery white carpet six inches deep.

Although the adults complained and set to work to clear the paths and byways, the children were delighted. Bundled up in woolen coats, scarves, and mittens, they ventured forth to make snowmen and snowballs. Their shrieks of excitement and happy chatter broke the stillness. For in comparison with the howling gales of the previous days the quiet calm of the snow-drenched landscape was strangely eerie.

And as if in acknowledgement of, and reverence for, the church-like atmosphere, news that the Grand Jury had issued indictments against three witches quietly circulated about the town. In muffled tones, and gestures common, the wary denizens of Boston town let their thoughts be known among their friends and relatives only.

About three weeks later, after a trial (petty) jury was convened, witnesses were summoned to testify and finally a report was issued after the bodies of the 'witches' had been thoroughly searched for marks or spots or other anomalies which were "insensible, and being pricked will not bleed." The marks of the Devil were supposedly found "in their secret parts and therefore required diligent and careful search," and when located proved that the women had indeed made "a league with the devil."

It was duly noted that the Reverend Cotton Mather was present at many of these trials stretching back for at least twenty years. He, it was, who offered advice to the judges and jury alike. And although he had urged vigorous prosecution of the devil's work, he also suggested a milder punishment than execution for the convicted witches.

Who was Cotton Mather?

From the pages of Mary Caroline Crawford's book, *Old Boston in Colonial Days,* we learn much of the Mathers' Dynasty – at least four generations of the family.

The Reverend Richard Mather is the first in line, as minister of Dorchester. He had a son named Increase, a young man theologically minded, born in June, 1639. Having given his first sermon on his birthday in 1657, Increase sailed for England to pursue post-graduate studies in Trinity College. He preached one winter in Devonshire and in 1659 became chaplain to the garrison of Guernsey.

However, in 1661, with the Restoration of the Monarchy, he was obliged to relinquish his charge, so he sailed for home. The next winter he alternated with his father in preaching to the New Church in the North-part of Boston.

In the spring of 1662, he married Maria Cotton, who was the only daughter of the celebrated Mr. John Cotton after whom he called his first-born son, John Cotton Mather.

Increase was ordained pastor of the North Church in Boston two years later and remained in that post for the next twenty years. A man of good sense and sound judgment, he exercised great influence in the temporal affairs of the colony as well as the spiritual. We are told that one of his most attractive traits was his "appreciation of his father." His motto in life seems to have been, "My Father can do no wrong..." From the pen of Barrett Wendell whose work *The Life of Cotton Mather* is "highly readable," we learn, "that the persecutor of the witches 'never observed any other law of God quite so faithfully as the Fifth Commandment.'"

This was the man who supported "the standard sequence of events in the courtroom. First the afflicted were questioned (and frequently suffered from fits, just as they had during the examinations). Then confessors were brought in; and next, witnesses to past acts of maleficium by the defendant were permitted to tell their stories. The results of searches for witch's marks would be presented, and finally the accused folk would offer whatever defense they could."[15]

Mary Beth Norton, "in analyzing the legal material" for her book, reached the following conclusions regarding the procedures carried out during the trials.

"First, most of the informal narratives prepared by the complaintants or their adult supporters, although they may have been read to the accused at examinations, were not later introduced into evidence in court. Very few such narratives have notations indicating they were presented to either grand or petty jury...

"Second, formal statements sworn at the grand-jury could also have been presented 'viva voce' to the petty jury... Third, and conversely, evidence labeled as 'sworn in court' but carrying no notation by the grand-jury foreman

---

15   Norton, Mary Beth. *In the Devil's Snare*. Alfred A. Knopf. New York, 2002. pg 207.

was probably not considered by that body. Since the petty jury sometimes heard cases a month or two after the grand-jury the prosecutor had time to recruit additional witnesses to fill in gaps in his case. Most documents in this category contain maleficium stories.

"Fourth, confessors probably appeared in most cases, testifying orally rather than in writing... Fifth, sworn testimony by adult supporters of the afflicted... carried great weight in the trials... Sixth, since criminal defendants were never allowed to swear to their innocence (for fear they would lie and endanger their immortal souls), exculpatory evidence was probably also not presented under oath and thus would not have been designated as 'sworn.'"[16]

The Reverend Cotton Mather's part in many of these trials can be summed up in his own words: "there was an extraordinary Endeavor by *witchcrafts*, with Cruel and frequent Fits, to hinder the poor Suffers from giving in their Complaints."

After such trials, the condemned was returned to prison to await public execution.

The Reverend "Cotton Mather went on to become the most celebrated clergyman in Massachusetts Bay, famed for his sermons and prolific writings. Late in life he was involved in another major controversy when he supported the efficacy of smallpox inoculations over the objections of prominent Boston physicians; his position was vindicated in the epidemic of 1722. He died in 1728, outliving his celebrated father, Increase, by only five years."[17]

---

16   Norton, Mary Beth. *In the Devil's Snare*. Alfred A. Knopf. New York, 2002. pg 208-209.
17   ibid pg.312

He was not only a Puritan clergyman, he was also a historian, and a pioneering student of science as well as a prolific writer. It was said of him that "he was both behind and ahead of his times. As an internationally known scholar and innovative scientist, he was ahead of his New England contemporaries. In his theories of child rearing, his emphasis on indirection, persuasion, and rewards considerably anticipated the future. But on questions of ecclesiastical organization and in all matters relating to Harvard College, of which his father, Increase, was nonresident president, he passionately adhered to past examples."[18]

18   *Encyclopedia of World Biography, 2ⁿᵈ Ed.* 17 vol. Gale Research, 1998.

Chapter 19

"The sure way to wickedness is always through wickedness."

- Seneca

The summer of 1688 had been a hot one. The children in the Goodwin household were particularly rambunctious as their governess had taken a vacation and they were left almost entirely on their own. From morning to night they raced through the house, up and down stairs, teasing the servants and in general making perfect nuisances of themselves. Their father was away on business and their mother, as was her wont, refrained from correcting them.

Then one morning as Ann Glover was folding and putting away some laundry in the upstairs cupboards, Martha, now thirteen, and the oldest daughter of the Goodwin family, came upon the servant. For some moments she watched quietly; then she noticed how carefully the washerwoman set aside some baby outfits. Martha knew these clothes had belonged to her baby sister Clotilde, who by this time had outgrown them.

Thinking only of her grandchild whom she knew would never know such finery, she decided to take the clothes the next day to the mistress and ask if she might have them.

Later that evening, Martha, who wasn't feeling too well, sought out her mother who lay resting on her favourite couch in her private sitting room.

"Mama, may I have a word with you," she politely asked when she entered into her mother's presence.

"Why, certainly, Martha. Come sit near me here," she answered pointing to a chair.

When Martha was seated, her mother again spoke, "Now, my dear, what is it you would talk to me about?"

"First of all, I think you should know that the washerwoman, Ann Glover, is stealing our clothes."

"Oh, Martha, Ann has been with us now for several years. She seems to be a decent sort of woman. Why would you accuse her of stealing clothes?"

"Well Mama, I saw her with my own two eyes today taking some of the baby clothes. I know Clotilde has outgrown them but still Ann Glover has no right to them."

"In that you are correct. But let us not jump to conclusions too hastily. Perhaps there were holes in them. Maybe the moths have got into them. We don't know yet what she intended to do, Martha, my dear."

"If she had intended to ask you for them, she would not have hidden them under her apron, Mama. I don't like that woman. She's Irish and Papist. Papa says all Papists are suspect and damned."

"I still think you may be jumping to conclusions, my dear. Now if you'll oblige me by handing me that glass of water, I'll be much obliged, child. Mama is tired and needs rest. It's time you had your supper."

Martha knew her mother had had enough so she left the room feeling somewhat rejected. Did her mother give more credence to a servant, a miserable one at that, than to her own daughter?

****

It started with a headache. Before she went to bed, Martha developed a bad headache. When she awoke the following morning she felt feverish. As she did not improve during the day, a physician was summoned. He prescribed liquids and cold towels. But as the day progressed, three other members of the family became ill. Again the physician was called and his diagnosis was "nothing but a hellish witchcraft could be the Origin of these maladies."

Immediately, Martha confirmed the doctor's diagnosis by claiming she became ill right after she caught Ann Glover stealing laundry.

Ann Glover was immediately arrested. Lodged in the local gaol, she protested, claiming innocence to the charges brought against her. She confessed that she had taken the clothes but had intended asking Madam Goodwin's permission before actually giving them to her granddaughter.

On the day of her imprisonment, the Reverend Cotton Mather visited her. His interviewing of her gave more torment than solace to the wretched woman.

"Confess to your sins and renounce the Papish religion which is so abominable in the sight of the Lord. Damnation awaits you if you cling to your old ways."

To these and all his other exhortations, Ann replied that she had no intention of giving up her faith.

"I'll go to my death, same as my husband, afore I'll be givin' up my Catholic religion," she shot back at the Puritan pastor. "An' don't you be tellin' me what is right and what is wrong, Sir."

Cotton Mather left shaking his head. He knew there was nothing he could do or say that would dissuade Ann 'Goody' Glover.

Two days later the court convened. Ann was brought before the judge and asked to account for her behaviour.

To all the questions asked of her, she refused to answer in the English language, but spoke only in Irish, her native language. Her manner and her determination only fueled the fire of hatred and resentment against her.

Again, according to Cotton Mather, "the court could have no answers from her, but in the Irish, which was her native tongue."

The court convicted her of witchcraft and sentenced her to be hanged. "She was drawn in a cart, a hated and dreaded figure, chief in importance, stared at and mocked at, through the principal streets from her prison to the gallows. The people crowded to see the end, as always. When it was over, they quickly dispersed, leaving the worn-out body hanging as a 'lesson' to evildoers." Thus did author James B. Cullen describe the end.

On November 16, 1688, Ann Glover was hanged.[19] Cotton Mather speaking at her trial said: "a scandalous old Irishwoman, very poor, a Roman Catholic and obstinate in idolatry."

---

19   In Boston's South End, Our Lady of Victories Eucharistic Shrine has a plaque commemorating Ann Glover as the first Catholic martyr of Massachusetts. The church is located at 27 Isabella Street. On November 16, 1988, the Boston City Council took note of the injustice done Ann Glover 300 years earlier by proclaiming that day "Goody Glover Day" and condemning what had been done to her.

Notes

1. It may be of interest to the reader to know that until about 1900 most Montserratans (Irish and Africans) spoke Irish Gaelic.

2. Montserratans know and accept that they descend from both Irish and African slaves.

3. Around 1868, a ship whose crew was Irish-speaking Cork-men dropped anchor at Montserrat. At the dock, the Irishmen were amazed to hear black Montserratans speaking Irish. The Montserratans even referred to Cork as *Corcaigh na gCuan* (Cork of the Harbours), a poetical term for Cork used by the Irish poets of ancient times but which had not been used in Ireland since the destruction of the Gaelic social system in the 17th century. Then the Montserratans, we are told, looked the Irishmen up and down and declared, *"Ta se sin ait, ni fheictear mar Gaeil sibh"* – "That's funny, you guys don't look Irish."

Ireland's Glorious Past

Many of my readers will not be aware of Ireland's glorious past. Therefore, I take the liberty to briefly outline the history of ancient Ireland, its culture and its contribution to Europe and the world.

The immense, mysterious monuments of Newgrange, Dowth and Knowth in the Valley of the Kings, just north of Dublin, date back to 3,500 BC and are man's earliest attempt to measure the passing year in accurate fashion. It was not the Middle East or China, as we are often led to believe, that gave birth to such an idea.

> "Ex oriente lux
> The light comes from the east?
> Yes, but from the west as well."

It was Plutarch who gave the name Ogygia to Ireland. It means 'most ancient,' thus giving evidence that Ireland was known and appreciated in bygone days.

"Were the Egyptian priests telling historical truth when they told Solon of Greece about the great civilization beyond the Pillars of Hercules?"[20]

I hope the short account I now pen of Ireland's history will in some small way clarify the enormity of the injustices suffered by the Irish for centuries in their own land by invading forces. But of greater importance, I hope it will show Ireland's true worth in spreading learning and culture not only in Europe, where the Irish were the saviors of Western Civilization, but throughout the world, through

20   Antpöhler, Werner. *Newgrange, Dowth, & Knowth.* Mercier Press, Cork, Ireland. 2000.

the sacrifices and efforts of thousands upon thousands of missionaries over hundreds of years.

Epilogue

"Breathes there a man with soul so dead,
Who never to himself hath said,
This is my own, my native land?"

- *Scott*

"Nature," says Gibbon, "has implanted in our breasts a lively impulse to extend the narrow span of our existence by the knowledge of the events that have happened on the soil which we inhabit, of the characters and actions of those men from whom our descent, as individuals or as a people, is probably derived. The same laudable emulation will prompt us to review and to enrich our common treasure of national glory; and those who are best entitled to the esteem of posterity are the most inclined to celebrate the merits of their ancestors."

"To know that myths teach the secret of things. In other words one learns not only how things came about but also where to find them and how to make them reappear when they disappear."

- Mircea Eliade, 1907

"The oldest existing literature of any people north of the Alps is the description of an assembly of ancient Irish stories collected and written about AD 1,100 by Irish monks and scribes. *The Book of Leinster* is the most well-known of all the volumes."[21]

---

21   Thomas, N.L. *Irish Symbols of 3,500 BC*. p. 79.

"Ireland was old when Greece and Rome were young."

- Dr. D Hyde

Sylvester O'Halloran, writing in the 1700s in his *History of Ireland,* compares Ireland's recorded past with other civilized and advanced nations of Europe. He points to the fact that countries like Greece and Rome were constantly harassed by invading armies, enemies wishing to destroy whatever advances those civilizations had achieved. Then he goes on to point out that the recorded accounts and chronology of these countries and even the Hebrews are uncertain at best. Varro, the most learned historian and philosopher of ancient Rome, according to O'Halloran, "deemed every relation which preceded the first Olympiad to be obscure, fabulous and unworthy of public notice."

O'Halloran then sets forth his detailed and undisputed account of Ireland's ancient past, "The nation, whose history I have the honor of presenting to the public, has experienced none of these misfortunes, at least not in so remarkable a degree as to destroy all her annals, or bring her chronology into any kind of doubt. They appear to have been, from the most remote antiquity, a *polished people*, and with propriety they may be called, *the fathers of letters!* Sequestered in a remote island, giving laws to neighbouring states and free from foreign invasions for the certain space of two thousand and sixty years, they had time and leisure to attend to their history and antiquities; and they certainly exceeded all nations of the world in their attention to these points."

Ancient Ireland's emergence from the mists of time is not always easy to trace. But we cannot reject what tradition and records have handed down; nor can we gloss over the in-depth studies of past historians whose writings are credible and whose assiduous pursuits of the truth led them to certain convictions regarding Ireland's first inhabitants. Though much of the country's ancient writings have been destroyed by those who would rob us of a glorious past, yet there is evidence not only from the old manuscripts which escaped the fires of bygone centuries, but also from the Continent of Europe, that such a past existed.

Ireland's Memory

Ireland's mythology is the oldest in Europe. Many myths and legends of days long past are still very much a part of the Irish psyche today. The Fo morians, one of the first people to inhabit the island, were also called the *Domnu,* meaning "the people of the deep sea." People who, according to the author Spence, came from Under the Sea, or from a country which had sunk beneath the waves: Atlantis![22]

Even to this day, the people of Ireland speak of *Tír na Nóg.* This land is always alluded to as being in the West, out in the mid-Atlantic.

The name Parthalon is the first to appear in the Irish history books. This leader came from Macedonia in Greece with about 1,000 followers. They remained in Ireland for about three centuries and then were wiped out by a plague. For thirty years the land was uninhabited, then a fresh colony came. These newcomers were related to the earlier Greeks and were under the leadership of Nemedius, who was eleventh in descent from Noah.

Next in line were the people called the Fo morians. "They lived," say the *Annals of Clonmacnoise,* "by piracy and plunder of other nations and were very troublesome to the whole world."

After the Fo morians came the *Firbolg*, descendents of the Nemedians who, having returned to Greece again, left that country some two hundred years later, arriving in Ireland about 1,300 BC. Another branch of the Nemedian

---

22   The author Teodor Gherasim in his book, *Atlantis – Lemuria and the Modern Connection,* states that in all probability, Ireland is an offshoot of that Lost Continent.

colony called the *Tuatha-De-Danann* arrived about the same time as *Fribolg*.

But of all the settlers, the most formidable were the Celts. Their coming to Ireland in about 1,000 BC has been well-documented.

The Phoenicians – the Celts

Dr. Villanueva has cleverly and convincingly traced the beginnings of the Irish race (the Celts) to the Phoenicians. In the opening pages of his work, *Phoenician Island*, he states: "It is greatly to be regretted that though no nation on the globe has been ever known to be more observant of its antiquities, nor more studiously careful of everything that could appertain to their chronology, the deeds of their ancestors, the boundaries of their jurisdictions, their laws, than this [Irish nation] has been, there should still appear such a mist of darkness spread before our path when we would investigate the origin of its primitive settlers. This obscurity is the more to be deplored from the character given by Camden of the Irish records, viz. that 'compared to them (the Irish) the antiquity of all other nations appeared as novelty and as it were the condition of incipient childhood.'"

Dr. Villanueva continues: "The extraordinary regard which the Scots-Milesians (Irish) like the Jews, paid to their history and the genealogy of their families, bespeaks a nation equally polished and educated. By a fundamental regulation of the state, it was necessary to prove connection with the royal house of Milesius before one could either ascend the throne, assume the sovereignty of any of the provinces, or be appointed to any capacity, military or magisterial. The office of the antiquarians, instituted by Ollamh Fodla, as part of the triennial council of the celebrated Tara, and whose duty it was to watch over those genealogies and perpetuate the memory of their houses, was under the strictest control of scrutinizing commissions appointed for that purpose, and the heaviest penalties were wont to be enforced against such as were found to prevaricate in the slightest particular. He enacted, besides, that copies of all registries which upon such examination were found pure, should be inserted in the great registry called the 'Psalter of Tara' and this practice and institution was continued and flourished up to the time of Christianity and long after."

The Celts

At its height in the 3rd century BC, the Celtic realm extended from the North Sea to the Mediterranean, and from the Black Sea to the Atlantic.

The Celts emerged as a distinct people in the 8th century BC – about the time Homer was composing the Iliad and the Odyssey, the Olympics were starting, and the legendary Romulus and Remus were founding Rome.

The Celts were energetic and most inventive. They introduced to Northern Europe the use of iron. Iron for tools and weapons, abundant, it was more efficient than bronze in felling men and forests, tilling the soil and providing transportation, etc. In seven centuries of cultural dominance, the Celts created Europe's first *major industrial* revolution, its first common market, its first international court of arbitration.

Celts introduced soap to the Greeks and Romans, invented chain armor, and were the first to shoe horses and give shape to handsaws, chisels, files, and other tools we use today.

They developed seamless iron rims for their wheels, set our standard 4 for 8 1/2 inch railroad gauge with the span of their chariots, and pioneered the iron plowshare and the rotary flour mill, a wheeled harvester two millennia before Cyrus McCormick. They also secured women's rights centuries before such a thing was dreamed of by other peoples.

Celts measured time not in days but in nights, divided months into a bright half and a dark half, and created an art style of such beauty that it endured 1,500 years. From their imagination emerged the Arthurian and Greek legends and the romance of Tristan and Iseult, *so* Celtic in its ardent beginning and tragic ending.

The entire map of Europe bears Celtic names. Rivers include Danube, Rhine, Seine, Thames, Shannon. Celtic settlements include London, Lyon, Geneva, Strasbourg, Bonn, Vienna, Budapest, Belgrade, Coimbra, Ankara. Paris recalls the Parisii, a Celtic tribe, and Rheims, the Remi.

Helvetia, poetic name for Switzerland, comes from the Helvetii, Belgium from the Belgae. The Bori descended into Italy, left their name in Bologna, and made their home in Bohemia.

To the Romans, the Celts were the Galli. The Gauls of Caesar's Gallic Wars were related to the Celts of Galicia in Spain and Poland and the Galatians in Asia Minor. So the Celts were not on the fringe but central to Europe's rise.

Irish and Greek Alphabets

The Cadmean letters of the Greeks and the Irish, in their
original order – The Greeks supposed to possess an occult
manner of writing – Figure of the Irish Ogham – Proofs and
reasons offered to show that, the Gadelian colony were the
first reformers of Greece.

Irish		Greek	
b,b	Beith.	B, β	Beta.
1,l	Luis.	Λ, λ	Lambda.
N,n	Nuin.	N, ν	Nu.
P,p	Poth.	Φ, φ	Phi.
S,ſ	Sail.	Σ, ς	Sigma.
δ,δ	Duir.	Δ, δ	Delta
ᚈ,ᚈ	Tinne.	T, τ	Tau.
C,ɔ	Colt.	K, κ	Kappa.
m,m	Muin.	M, μ	Mu.
ᚌ,ᚌ	Gort.	Γ, γ	Gamma.
R,ſ	Ruis.	P, ρ	Rho.
ꝺ,a	Ailim.	Λ, α	Alpha.
O,o	On.	O, o	Omicron.
u,u	Uillean.	Υ, υ	Upsilon.
e,ε	Eadha.	E, θ	Eta.
J,j	Jodha.	I, ι (probaby the ancient)	Iota.

Besides this alphabet, the early Greeks, we have reason to suspect, had also an occult manner of writing, like our Ogham, or sacred character. For Pausanias says, that the coffer of Cypselus, preserved in the city of Elis, had on it inscriptions in old characters, and straight lines. We shall exhibit a scheme of our Ogham, correspondent with the alphabet; as it may probably elucidate this remarkable passage of Pausanias.[23]

---

23   O'Halloran Silvester, *The History of Ireland,* chapter 5, Dublin, 1774

Characteristics of the Celts

Love of fashion, talk, freedom; dreamers, artists, lovers of poetry, story telling and music.

The Irish story of the Brown Bull of Cualnge has been described as the wonder and most fascinating saga not only of the entire Celtic world but even of all Western Europe.

Culture – The Wonder of the Western World

The degree of civilization of the people of Ireland during the last centuries BC and the first centuries AD was very advanced, so much so indeed, that the combination of the established Iron Age culture with the new ideas which Christianity brought in its train rendered inevitable the development of an art and a spiritual mission which were destined to become in time *the Wonder of the Western World.*

The Celts of Ireland

Historians of old have given various names to Ireland. Diodorus Siculus gave it the name Irin. Strabo and after him, Claudian, called the land Ierna, and Ptolemy, Juverna and Orpheus of Cortona used the name Iernia. Later Hibernia, signifying a western country, was used. Some, however, say the name derived from Heber, one of the sons of Milesius; while others affirm that the word is of Pheonician origin and means 'the remotest habitation.'

For many ages, down to the eleventh century, Ireland bore the name of Scotia, a name which is derived from a Scythian source, signifying that the Scythians were among the first inhabitants. But others think that the name Scotia comes from Scota, the wife of Gadelius, a lady reputed to be the daughter of Pharaoh.

The Milesians

No one knows for sure what the boundaries of Ancient Scythia were. Nor do we know from what great branch of the human family the Scythians sprang.

In the time of Heroditus, they were spread across Europe along the Danube to the Caucasus. They were a pastoral people and their bravery in battle none could withstand.

In time, we learn the names of some of the leaders. Niall, son of Feniursa is one. His father is said to have known all languages. Niall eventually settled in Egypt, married Scota, the daughter of Pharaoh, and obtained a principality by the shores of the Red Sea. Befriending Moses and the persecuted Israelites, he evoked the enmity of Pharaoh, who drove him and his followers from their home. Forced to flee, Niall traversed North Africa. Then after several hundred years, his descendants arrived in Spain under the leadership of Milesius.

An old Druid had long foretold that the Milesians or followers of Milesius as these Phoenicians were now known, would one day possess a far-off Western isle. To Ireland, they therefore resolved to go. The historian, Keating, states that they landed in the year 1,300 BC. The number of ships was thirty, each holding thirty of the most courageous of their troops, their wives, and many followers. Thus did the Celts, as they were now called, inhabit Ireland.

The country was from this time forth ruled by kings and princes until well into the 14th century AD. One of the first kings was Ollamh. This name means professor, testifying that he was a man of letters and as such he did everything he could to encourage learning. "Anxious to have good laws passed, and to have besides the records of the kingdom accurate, and trustworthy, he assembled, every third year at his palace in Tara, an assembly of the princes, druids, bards, and other learned men of the kingdom; public affairs were then discussed, new laws enacted, old laws, if useless or injurious, repealed. The records of the kingdom were carefully examined and criticized, whatever was deemed inaccurate was expunged, due corrections were made, and thus corrected these records were handed down to posterity as authentic history."[24]

During the joint reign of Cimbaeth and his wife Macha, the place of Emania near Armagh was built. This was a seat of learning and much influence throughout the whole land.

King Ugaine was the first monarch to be called Great. "Not content with the sovereignty of Ireland, he went over the sea to France, where his arms were ever victorious, until at length he ruled over all Western Europe."[25]

Other names are recorded, among them, Conn of the Hundred Battles, but the king who was considered the best was Cormac MacArt. He reigned in the third century AD. He held regular meetings of the Feis of Tara, enacted many

24   D'Alton, Rev. E.A. *History of Ireland.* The Gresham Publishing Co. London. 1912. (Vol. 1, pg. 18-19).
25   Ibid. pg 19.

wise laws, carefully corrected the Psalter of Tara and even wrote a book called *Princely Institutions.* He became a Christian and thereby embittered the Druids.

This might be a good place to list some of the laws, more Democratic than any others in the world of the time, which were drawn up by the Druids and followed throughout the land.

The Brehon Laws[26]

According to Seamus MacManus, a popular historian of the 20th century, the great body of ancient Irish law, still existing in five large volumes – the principal part of these being the *Senchus Mor* – is an amazing and beautiful work admired by jurists and laymen alike.

In this vast body of the old Irish laws almost every conceivable relationship, social and moral, between men, women and children exists.

Some examples will suffice to show how far beyond the societies of the rest of the world the Irish culture and civilization had advanced. In the *Senchus Mor* we have laws dealing with all kinds of bargains, contracts and

---

26   Brehon – A legal expert who devoted himself or herself to arbitration and was paid a fee by his client – more than a judge. In studying for this profession, the Brehon had not only to become master of the ancient legal records but he must also be a genealogist and historian – 8-10 years study!

engagements between men and women as well as men with men.

1. Laws respecting Property...
2. Laws respecting Gifts, Alms, and Endowments...
3. Laws as to Waifs, Strays, Derelictions...
4. Laws concerning the relation of father and son, or illegitimate children; adoption and affiliations...
5. Laws minutely regulating the Fees of Doctors, Judges, Lawyers and Teachers, and of all other professional persons.
6. A series of laws concerning the varied species of Industry: such as Weaving, Spinning, Sewing, Building, Brewing, etc.; concerning Mills and Weirs; concerning Fishing; concerning Bees, Poultry etc.

And the lists continue.

Regarding Women, the laws were far in advance of any others in any part of the world. From the remotest time, Ireland above all the nations of the world held her women-folk in high regard. Women were emancipated, eligible for the professions, for rank and fame.

Before a Brehon court, a wife and husband were equal. Marriage was a contract between two equals – the woman always maintaining herself and her personal possessions without question of confiscation by the husband.

"In Ireland, after marriage, the woman did not become a chattel – thus radically differing from the usual custom in the other countries of Europe. Before marriage she was wooed and courted like the superior being which, later, she was acknowledged to be in all countries. In the exercise of the acknowledged privileges of a superior being she could scorn and frown down the attentions of chieftains and kings – and scholars too – send them home with hanging heads, and choose whomsoever her heart went out to."[27]

Christianity and the Golden Age of Ireland

The Roman soldiers conquered all of Western Europe as far as the border between England and Alba (Scotland) where they erected the Hadrian Wall to keep the 'savages' at bay. The only country never occupied by the Romans was Ireland. Consequently, with the coming of Christianity and the advanced Irish culture and civilization, Ireland became the reservoir of learning for the entire Continent. Science, music, art, mathematics, philosophy, literature of the known world, languages including Greek and Latin all were taught in the schools, universities and monasteries which abounded throughout the country. With the fall of the Roman Empire and the resulting devastation to learning across the Continent, Ireland became Europe's salvation.

The noble and upper classes left in Europe, realizing what Ireland had to offer, sent their youth to study and be

27   MacManus, Seamus. *The Story of the Irish Race*. The Devin-Adair Company. Old Greenwich, Connecticut. 1979. pg 154.

educated in the Irish schools. There they were housed, taught and fed free of charge.

But Ireland's contribution to the saving of Western Civilization did not end there. The monks, nuns, professors and other educators set out on a mission to restore that civilization. All across Europe they went setting up schools and universities, from Iona in Scotland through England, France and Germany to as far away as Kiev in the Ukraine. Bobbio in Italy, and St. Gall in Switzerland are but two of these universities which were founded by the Irish and are still operating today.

Many have written of Ireland's remarkable men and women. The Saxon Aldhelm wrote, "Ireland is a fertile and blooming nursery of letters: one might reckon the stars of heaven, as enumerate her students and literature." The German Professor Zimmer states, "They [the Irish] laid the cornerstone of Western culture on the Continent, the rich result of which Germany shares and enjoys today, in common with all other civilized nations." And again, in his work *The Irish Element in Mediaeval Culture*, Zimmer states, "Ireland can indeed lay claim to a great past; she can not only boast of having been the birthplace and abode of high culture in the fifth and sixth centuries, at a time when the Roman Empire was being undermined by the alliances and inroads of German tribes, which threatened to sink the whole Continent into barbarism, but also of having made strenuous efforts in the seventh and up to the tenth century to spread her learning among the German and Romance peoples, thus forming the actual foundation of our present continental civilization."

From Professor Sandy in his work entitled *History of Classical Scholarship* come the following words: "The

Latin poet, Sedulius, [Seadhal] the Christian Virgil, and the noted Roman lawyer, Celestius [Cellah] were all Irish. The renaissance began in Ireland seven hundred years before it was known in Italy."

Many more have written regarding Ireland's contribution to Europe and the rest of the world. Countless missionaries from the time of St. Patrick, fifth century, down to our own day, have left home and country and spent their lives in foreign lands all across the globe teaching, preaching and bringing culture and civilization to millions.

The Coming of the Vikings

The Viking invasions, not only in Ireland but all over Europe, caused devastation of property and great loss of life. The Vikings of Norway and Denmark were chiefly responsible for the havoc and destruction to Ireland's schools, monasteries and royal castles throughout the land. They began their exploits as early as the eighth century and continued to plunder, destroy and kill or capture young men and maidens for the next two hundred years. Those captured were usually sold as slaves on the Continent of Europe, while the clergy, the monks and nuns were invariably killed and their dwelling places burned to the ground. The valuables housed within – gold chalices and other vessels used in the Catholic services – were carried off to their *drekars* – dragon ships, and taken back to their homes or sold in the trading posts on the Baltic Sea.

It wasn't until King Brian Boru in 1014 claimed a decisive victory over the Vikings at the Battle of Clontarf that the power of these marauders was finally broken and Europe as well as Ireland freed from their savage exploits.

However, two hundred years of periodic attacks wrought havoc on the country. Nor did Ireland ever again get the opportunity to completely recover. For as soon as the Vikings were conquered, the English invasions began and never ceased until the 20th century. Thus was a culture and a civilization far in advance of all others in Western Europe brought low. The 'Island of Saints and Scholars' was torn apart. And as we have seen in the 1600s, so crushed was Ireland that a large number of its citizens were carried off as slaves to the American Colonies and the West Indies. In the 1700s the schools were closed. No Irishman or woman could attain an education. The Sovereign of England would keep the Irish not only poor but ignorant. Only those who could afford passage to the Continent gained an education. But they went in droves and eventually many made their way back to teach in what have been called the 'Hedge Schools.' Under the weather, in nooks and crannies, they gathered the children and under pain of death sought to give them some form of education.

Thus was Ireland once a proud, noble and distinguished country; a land of learning, of laws far in advance of any other society, brought to its knees. And that by those whom it had helped instruct and elevate to the higher things of life – England.

Bibliography

Crawford, Mary Caroline. *Old Boston in Colonial Days.* L.C Page and Co. 1908.

D'alton, Rev. E.A. *History of Ireland.* The Gresham Publishing Co. London. 1912.

Danckaerts, Jasper. *Journal.* Charles Scribner's Sons. New York. 1913.

Drake, Ross, Marjorie. *The Book of Boston.* Hastings House Publishers. New York. 1960.

Jennings, John. *Boston Cradle of Liberty.* Doubleday & Company, Inc. Garden City, NY. 1947.

MacManus, Seamus. *Story of the Irish Race.* The Devlin-Adair Company. Old Greenwich, Connecticut. 1979.

Villanueva. J.L. *Phoenician Ireland.* Translated by Henry O'Brien. London. 1833.

About the Author

Born and raised in Ireland, Lousie Gherasim came to this country in the 1950's. She is a successful novelist, writing for adults, teenagers, and children.

Her love and understanding of the Irish people – their history, their struggles, their indomitable spirit and undying attachment to their native land, its art, music and literature, lends to her writing something of the strength of her rich Gaelic heritage.

About the Artist

Neecol Johnson is an Oregon artist who through her painting tells a story combining both impressionism and realism. Her art media include Ink Drawing, Oils, Pastels, and Watercolor.